Angels At Play

Michael Howard

Copyright © 2011

Michael Howard

All rights reserved.

ISBN: **097690151X**
ISBN-13: **978-0976901518**

Previous Editions:
On The Head Of A Pin – Copyright 1998
Angels On Assignment – Copyright 2003

DEDICATION

To my mother, Vernelda Bueno, who taught me to believe in myself and how to spell.

To my friends and coworkers, in the "Cubicle Maze," who encouraged me in this project without really understanding where it was going or why I was doing it.

But most of all, to my late wife Linda, who encouraged me, prodded me, proofread for me, and loved me throughout the process of writing this book. The vow should read "Till death do we part, or until he decides to be an author."

"We are not physical beings having a spiritual experience. Rather we are spiritual beings having a physical experience."

Teilhard DeChardin, French philosopher

PREFACE

The Preface of a book is usually a place for the author to prepare you for the story that is to follow. It sets the stage. It draws you in.

But I feel that a good Preface should actually do more than that. It should also answer some very obvious, and often overlooked, questions. It should tell me things I want to know before I turn another page of any book I read.

So let's get right down to it. Why did I write this book? With plenty of books in print, all of them begging for your attention and your dollars, why did I take the time to put my words on paper?

The answer is simple. I had to.

Every book you read is an author's attempt to share something of his or her own universe with you. Whether the book is poetry or prose, fiction or non, the author has opened themselves up to let you see their truth.

I was driven to share my truth with you. I felt an undeniable need to make this story available to you, to let you see what the universe looks like from my perspective.

In a moment, when you begin to read Chapter 1, you will be starting on an adventure that just may stretch your way of thinking about your universe. I sincerely hope that it will challenge your ideas. I know that it challenged many of mine, even as I wrote it.

You may relate to everything in this book, part of it, or nothing. Please feel free to accept what you like and ignore what you don't. Try to remember that two precious gifts which we all have in common are our uniqueness and our free will.

So now, without further ado, I welcome you into my reality, and hope that you enjoy what you experience there.

Michael Howard

Chapter 1

"Another perfect day, but then again, they all are, aren't they?" I said with a smile.

It was a typical Monday morning in our cubicle maze and my unusual comment was rewarded with a few strange looks from the coworkers who had dropped by to see me. It also drew a low murmur of "Pollyanna!" from someone in another cubicle, followed by a chuckle from everyone else in earshot.

I'd just gotten back from a long needed vacation and was in better spirits than any of my friends had ever seen. In fact, it was probably the best mood I'd ever experienced.

My over-the-wall neighbor, Dean, popped his head up and added, "Well, we know what he did while he was gone!" This resulted in louder chuckles.

I just laughed along, but knew that they had no idea. I would have to go over it in my own mind first, before I could even hope to get anyone to understand. Even my wife seemed be having trouble accepting my story.

What had been planned as a week of reflection and relaxation had turned into much, much more.

Chapter 2

My wife and I were doing something we had never done before, taking separate vacations. She was to attend a seminar for Spa Managers and Owners in Salt Lake City. I was going on a "personal retreat" at a place called Breitenbush, just east of Salem, Oregon.

We flew together to Dallas, but parted ways when her flight left out of American Airlines gate 34. With my flight departing out of gate 14, a full concourse away, and having three hours to kill, I decided to take a leisurely stroll and window shop the airport stores.

I never cease to be amazed at the stuff they try to sell in airports these days; everything from live cacti to assorted jalapeno sauces. Most of it is overpriced junk and souvenir trinkets, but one small shop display was actually different.

This one had books, statues, T-shirts, and posters, like all the others, but was dedicated entirely to angel designs. They even had Gummy Angels, "the Heavenly treat."

A lady of 60-ish, who seemed totally unaffected by the rush and turmoil of the airport outside her door, ran the shop. She smiled and greeted everyone who came in, taking the time to chat when someone asked about an item or commented about the store.

When I finally walked inside, there was no one else around, and she was busily dusting some of the shelves in the back with an old fashioned feather duster. Hearing me enter, she turned and called "Come on in, dear," and stuffed the duster into a pocket of the lacy white apron that she wore over her blue flowered dress. She then went through a curtained doorway into the back room.

As I browsed about, my attention was soon drawn to a pin that was displayed in a glass case. While the case held dozens of pins, lockets, rings, and pendants, of various qualities and designs, all involving angels, this one really jumped out at me.

It was the figure of a golden angel with a sword, which was incredibly detailed, and almost seemed to glow. I was mesmerized by it.

"That's Michael," the shopkeeper said from behind me, startling me a bit, "and I'm Clara, to my friends. And any friend of Michael's is a friend of mine."

"Oh, uh, hi." I replied, surprised and a bit embarrassed at being so engrossed in a piece of jewelry. "I'm sorry. I didn't hear you walk up. That pin is really beautiful."

"Yes, very lovely, and 18-karat gold," she said with a smile. She had a slight accent (Irish maybe?). "Some say he's God's policeman. I guess that's why they always have him holding a sword. It makes him look more fierce than he really is."

"Where are you off to today, business or pleasure?" she continued quickly, changing the subject in a way that seemed strangely awkward. It was like she had just said something she didn't mean to.

"Pleasure, this time. A little resort in Oregon called Breitenbush."

"Central Oregon," she bubbled, "how lovely! Mountains and trees and rivers!"

"Do you know of Breitenbush?" I asked, rather surprised again. "Have you been there?"

"Well, not Breitenbush, but near there. My friend, Ariel, and I stay at a place called Pinhead Buttes, northeast of there. They have a wonderful lodge, with a spectacular view and a hot spring. A lot of really special people go there."

"Well, I'll have to keep my eyes open for it." I said, checking my watch and wondering what she meant by "special people."

"Oh, you have plenty of time. Here!" She said, smiling and holding out a small box.

"What?" I gasped, suddenly realizing that she had packaged up the pin while we were talking. "But how much is it?"

She pressed the box into my hand, and clasped it closed with both of hers, saying "Don't worry about it, dear. I think Michael was supposed to fly with you today."

"Won't your boss get mad about you giving things away?"

"No," she grinned, "she would want you to have it. Stop by on your way back and tell me about your trip."

"Okay, I will. And, thanks, Clara," I replied, as she gave a little wave and turned to talk to another customer, who had entered without my notice.

Normally I don't like to wear jewelry, but for some reason I decided to put the little angel pin on. After attaching it to my lapel, I realized that I'd spent enough time in the shop that I needed to jog the last few gates to make my plane.

Chapter 3

Breitenbush is a secluded "resort" located north of Detroit, Oregon, due east of Salem. It is communally owned, so that anyone who works there for a year becomes a part owner for as long as they stay.

The area surrounding the resort is mostly old-growth forest, with a scattering of bald spots that are the result of clear-cut logging.

All in all, it is one of the most beautiful places on earth. Just like Clara said, trees and mountains and rivers.

For the visitor, Breitenbush offers hot mineral water bathing, hiking trails, vegetarian cuisine, massage services, and seminars on topics from Yoga to Primal Drumming. It's sort of a natural health version of Disneyland.

The key things to remember about a stay at Breitenbush are: don't forget to make a reservation and secure it with a deposit; the cabins are somewhat rustic, with some actually having attached bathrooms; and don't be surprised if you find yourself wanting to join the staff, rather than going back to your regular job. I learned these things on my previous visit, five years earlier.

After leaving Dallas, my flight was uneventful, except for a couple of compliments on my new traveling companion, Michael, from the flight attendants. Since he was the strong silent type, I thanked them for him. When *we* arrived in Portland, my rental car was waiting. The four-hour drive was even more scenic that I had remembered. On reaching the parking lot at Breitenbush, I was a bit disappointed to see that it was almost full. I had been hoping that this would be a slow week for them, making it easier for me to find secluded places to call my own.

As I walked the hundred or so yards to the office, I saw that there were people everywhere. "They must be having some sort of large seminar," I thought. "Maybe they'll be in class all day and I can at least have the run of the place while they're otherwise involved."

When I got to the office, however, the outlook changed from bleak, to dark, to black. Not only were all these people here on "personal retreats," but, while they were very sorry, my reservation seemed to have been written down for the following week.

There was, in short, no room at the inn.

Not being the type to give up, I asked about the dormitories. "No, full." How about the campground, could they rent me a tent? "No." Could I sleep in a classroom, or maybe in one of the residents' houses? "NO! And that's final."

Disappointed, I got back in my car, trying to remember if I had seen any other lodging on the way up. I was beginning to think that this trip was going to be a disaster and that I would be reporting back to Clara sooner than I had hoped.

"Clara!" I said out loud, pulling the map out of the glove box. "What was the name of her resort, Pinhead Buttes?"

I found nothing on the map that looked anything like that, but, following a hunch (and, since real men never stop and ask directions) I pulled out of the Breitenbush parking lot, heading north.

Sure enough, several miles up the road there was a small sign, white with blue lettering, "Pinhead Buttes Resort - Private Drive."

"Private Drive?" I wondered as I pulled to a stop at the bottom of a narrow road, which headed up the mountain. "Does that mean for everyone to keep out, as in, "Members Only," or is it just to keep the non-guest riffraff from driving up?"

Since the worst they could do would be to tell me to leave, I put the car back in gear and started up the mountain.

Almost as soon as the car was moving, I began to see why Clara loves this place. I noticed that the forest actually got thicker as I drove, and was amazed at how much more beautiful it got the further I went.

Suddenly, a herd of seven or eight deer ran out of the woods, causing me to brake hard to avoid them. They ran a few yards into the trees on the other side of the road and then stopped to see what I was going to do. It was as if they were totally unafraid of me.

"You better not do that around hunters," I warned them, and then wondered how they could be so fearless.

After a few minutes of watching the deer watch me, I continued up the road and they went on about their business.

By the time I reached the top of the mountain, it was beginning to get dark. This was actually good because it allowed me to see the lodge at Pinhead Buttes in its absolute glory as I arrived.

Chapter 4

Clara's "wonderful lodge" was somewhat more than that. It was spectacular; it was awesome! It had a look that promised magic and mystery.

The structure had three floors, with a tower gracing the front corner, and was made of a material that looked like marble. Its arched portals and covered walkways reminded me of some of the old Spanish missions that I had visited in California when I was younger.

The most magical aspect, however, was the glow. The entire lodge was bathed in an even white light, apparently from carefully positioned floodlights, making it seem to shine from within. This was an effect that I had never seen done so perfectly.

As I drove toward the corner of the building that appeared to be the main lobby entrance, I realized that there were two things conspicuously missing. There weren't any kind of signs, either to identify the building or to direct the guests where to go to check-in. There was also no evidence of where to park your car when you got there.

In fact, there were no other cars in sight. I did not even see another exit from the circular driveway that could lead to a hidden parking area.

I began to wonder if the lodge was closed. Surely, they didn't want guests to park on the large, well-manicured lawn that filled the clearing in front of the lodge?

I parked the car at the bottom of the steps and got out, mentally bracing myself for the rejection or the locked door that I would probably find at the top.

Now that the sun had set, the mountain air had become chilly, so I dug a light coat out of my one carry-on bag. I then hefted the bag's strap onto my shoulder and started up the steps.

There were two things that I really liked about the lodge's main lobby doors, they were of carved glass, not etched, with detailed images of birds and flowers in them (must have cost a fortune!); and, more important, they were unlocked.

As I entered the huge lobby, which was notably absent of the usual stuffed wildlife that is almost universally found in mountain lodges, I also realized that I still had not seen any people. Were they all in some meeting or dining room? There should be at least a desk clerk.

I approached what appeared to be the main desk, a large counter of beautifully carved light oak, and noticed a golden desk bell. Before I could ring it, two men came out of an office behind the desk.

This first man, who looked at me as if I was a vagrant who had just asked to marry his daughter, seemed to be of the snobbish, formal British butler type that you would see in old movies. He was dressed in a starched white shirt, a dark blue blazer, and a tie.

His companion, who was dressed the same, but seemed to be more friendly, smiled and nodded when he saw me. He then went about some other business behind the desk.

"May I help you, sir?" said the first in a frigid tone that indicated that he had absolutely no intention of doing so.

"Yes," I replied, trying to be businesslike but friendly. "I was wondering if you have any vacancies for tonight."

"I'm sorry, sir," he snorted, "but this is a very exclusive resort. You must be a member, or be referred by one, to stay here. Besides, we currently have no vacancies." He emphasized the last few words by tapping his finger on the desk in cadence with them and staring fiercely into my eyes.

"But surely you have something...anything."

I was beginning to beg. That just isn't how to handle these types, although they love it. I had to figure a way to get him to help me. A place this big could not have a lobby this empty and still have no rooms left.

"Look," I continued, setting down my bag and removing my coat. "I came all the way from Oklahoma. The resort where I was planning to spend the week was full up and I need a place to stay, at least for tonight. Could you please help me?"

I glanced at the other clerk, who was now staring at me. His eyes were wide with surprise. He walked over and placed his hand on the snobbish one's shoulder, to get his attention.

"Just a minute, Simon," he said testily, glancing at his coworker and then turning back to me.

"Now, sir, you can't expect…" he started.

His eyes were now wide and Simon was whispering urgently in his ear, "No, look!"

"…us to turn you away under these circumstances. I'm sure we can accommodate you, sir. A week, you say? Why, yes, we have a very nice room on the third floor with a valley view." He had changed gears with only a slight pause, but now he kept looking at my lapel instead of in my eyes.

He tapped the bell and a tall teenager in a similar blazer appeared.

"Take this gentleman to room 3260, Lawrence," he instructed the youth, handing him a key.

To me he said, "My name is Thomas, if you need anything. Anything at all."

Now he was almost groveling, but why? I hadn't changed, why did he?

I followed the bellman through the lobby to the elevator, marveling at the opulence of it all. This wasn't a lodge; it was a first-class hotel.

In the center of the lobby was a large sunken conversation pit, with comfortable looking padded seats in a circle around its rim. In the center stood a twelve-foot tall carved crystal statue of an angel with its wings slightly spread.

The angel stood on a marble pedestal that was dome shaped, but made with layers of varying shade and size, creating a series of small circular ledges. Over these ledges flowed water that came from around the feet of the statue, making a musical waterfall sound as it fell into a pool that surrounded the whole structure.

As amazing as this fountain would normally be, it too was somehow lit by hidden spotlights so that it seemed to glow from within.

Whoever built this place was a master at the use of light and shadow.

The rest of the lobby was just as spectacular, with statuary everywhere, all with that same luminous quality to it, all done with exquisite detail.

The elevator had polished light oak wood paneled doors, with inlaid golden figures of two angels, one on each door, leaning inward with their wing tips touching when the doors were closed.

Although the building was massive, it actually took the form of an open square, with a large garden enclosed inside. This garden, though completely hidden from someone outside of the building, could be seen in all of its glory from the glass elevators that carried guests to the upper floors. These elevators were located in each corner of the central garden courtyard.

As we boarded the elevator, I once again noticed the lack of signs, not even a poster in the elevator for the dining room.

"Lawrence, was it?" I asked as the elevator door closed and I could still see the two desk clerks staring after us.

"Yes, sir?" the bellman replied, trying not to stare at me.

"Is there any place to get something to eat around here?"

"Yes sir. There's a dining room on the first floor, to your left through the lobby. It will be open for another two hours, at least. Your meals come with the room."

"Thanks," I said as the door opened and we stepped out onto the third floor.

"The second and third floors are entirely guest rooms." Lawrence began, by way of an orientation, while leading me to my room in the far corner of the building. "The first floor is all dining, meeting rooms, shops, and recreation. We have a small movie theater, a gym, a library, and a chapel. The aviary is above the courtyard garden. In the basement are a small bowling alley, a swimming pool, a spa, and the Grotto."

"And what is this Grotto?" I asked.

"Oh, it's an underground hot spring. It bubbles up into a natural cavern under the resort. The rock seats can be a little hard on the bottom, but it's well worth it."

"To get there you just take the elevator to the basement and follow the hall to the left. At the end of the first wing, you'll find a metal spiral staircase that goes down into the cavern."

"There's also an observation tower directly above the lobby. Just take the stairs up from this floor, right across the hall from the lobby elevator."

"Here we are, sir, room 3260." He concluded, as we reached a door in the northeast corner of the third floor, just across from another elevator.

"How can you tell," I wondered out loud. "There are no numbers on any of the rooms."

"Oh, you just know," he replied with a grin. "You'll see what I mean. When you allow yourself, don't you always find your way to where you were meant to be?"

He opened the door, stepped aside to let me enter, and then followed me in, carrying my bag.

After he set the bag down, something akin to a miracle occurred; he turned and started out of the door, without pausing to wait for a tip.

"Good night, Sir. Call if you need anything." And he stepped into the hall.

"Uh, Lawrence," I called, reaching into my pocket, as he was about to close the door.

"Thank you, sir, but no. We're fully compensated by the management for our work. Tipping isn't allowed from Members. Thanks anyway." And he was gone.

"Oh, so now I'm a member," I thought, and started to explore my home for the next few days.

Chapter 5

Room 3260 was actually a suite. It had a living room, bedroom, kitchenette, and bathroom.

The living room was opulent, with a couch, mini-bar, 60-inch television, stereo, and writing desk. It was done up in sky-blue, off-white, and gold-trim, pretty much the color scheme for most of the rest of the resort.

The kitchenette was fully equipped and actually stocked with a basic food supply. This included a variety of soft drinks and imported beers in the refrigerator.

The bathroom had a 6-foot sunken whirlpool tub, with gold fixtures, set into a glass block pedestal. There was also a massive, walk-in closet, a shower, and a full supply of toiletries.

The topper was the bedroom. A small gold and crystal chandelier hung from the center of a robin's egg blue ceiling. The bed was a king size canopy type, with gold posts, white and blue curtains and bedspread. Along the wall were a white antique chest of drawers with gold-leaf trim, another big screen TV, and a bookcase.

As I wandered back into the living room, I began to think about the price, which was never mentioned when I checked in. In most hotels they have a little sign on the back of the room door that tells you the important stuff that you might forget, or be too embarrassed, to ask the desk clerk. Things like your room number, what the checkout time is, and how much this place will set you back.

True to form for Pinhead Buttes, there was no such sign.

Well, I needed to go down and move my car away from the steps anyway, so I decided to get some dinner, tour the facilities, and save the shock to my bank account for last. If it came down to a choice of staying just the one night or taking out a second mortgage on the house, I would just have to move on in the morning.

On my way back to the lobby side elevator, I took time to look at some of the artwork on the hallway walls. It was all amazing and, while I am not a great scholar of fine arts, I recognized some of them as very good replicas of famous works. I don't refer to them as prints because they had that smell and brushed texture of real oil paintings.

The hallway itself had gold and blue carpeting, light oak wainscoting, white wallpaper with blue and gold flowers, and a robin's egg blue ceiling, with gold-leaf molding. Lighting for the hallways came from indirect lighting hidden in the molding at the ceiling level, but gave a much more even illumination than I had ever seen before.

I took the elevator down to the first floor, enjoying the view of the garden with its lighted paths and waterfalls, and re-entered the lobby.

To get to the dining room, I had to pass the front desk. Now there was a different clerk on duty. She was about forty, attractive, and wore a slightly more feminine version of the same uniform that Simon and Thomas had worn earlier.

The hallway leading to the dining room was more ornate that those on the upper floors, but had the same color scheme, design, and abundance of artwork.

I was greeted at the door of the dining room by the first two signs that I had seen on the property. The first, in gold block lettering on an oval shaped sky-blue background was located above the entrance and read "San Miguel's." The other, attached to the receptionist's podium, stated "Buffet Tonight - Please help yourself."

I saw no staff and no other guests, so I took the sign's suggestion.

The buffet was an open invitation to gluttony. As anyone who has seen my waistline knows, I have an intimate relationship with food. Believe me, this was an outstanding buffet.

Unlike what I would have eaten at Breitenbush, this was not restricted to the vegetarian palate. No, far from it. If it is edible, it was probably on that buffet, if not on that first night, then on one of the others.

I won't bore you with a bite-by-bite replay, but it was beyond good.

Leaving San Miguel's, I once again began to wonder about the other guests. After all, I had still only seen a total of four people, all of whom were staff.

Well, earlier at Breitenbush I had been disappointed by too many people, why should I be upset now about too few? Because it was very odd, especially after being told there were no vacancies.

Was that just a snobbish lie? Then, why his change of heart? What made the other clerk, Simon, look so surprised?

I was asking myself these questions as I walked back into the lobby and sat down on one side of the conversation pit to admire the crystal angel.

It took me a moment, but I soon became aware that I was not alone by the statue. There was also a couple in their early thirties, with a little blonde girl of about three, on the other side.

The little girl was wearing a pretty blue dress, with white lace at the collar, and a gold belt, and was standing right at the edge of the pond. She was holding her mother's hand, pointing at the statue, and saying something over and over.

At first, I couldn't make out the word she was saying, but as I moved a little closer, I realized that she kept repeating the name "Michael."

Her parents noticed me, and the mother tried to hush the little girl. "Now, Tootsie, you're bothering that man."

"No, that's OK," I told them, "she's not bothering me. You have a beautiful daughter."

I introduced myself, and they told me that they were Gene and Alameda, and that their daughter was Linda.

There was something familiar about them, but I couldn't place it at the time.

Gene told me that they had to go, and they were out the front door without another word.

Their leaving reminded me that my car was still parked by the front steps, so I walked over to the desk to ask where I should put it.

"Excuse me," I said to the desk clerk, and introduced myself.

"Yes, sir. I'm Barbara," she replied. "How can I help you?"

"Well, before I checked in, I didn't see where we were supposed to park our cars. There were no signs or anything, so I left it parked in front of the door. Where do I need to move it?"

"Room number, sir?" she asked and then turned to the rows of mail slots on the back wall.

When she came back, she handed me my car key, which I had thought was still in my pocket. We took the liberty of parking it for you, sir. You seem to have left the key in it. Will there be anything else?"

"No. Thank you," I said, and turned back toward the angel.

The angel. Michael? Of course, he was holding a sword, just like my pin. In fact, I realized, pulling up my lapel to look at my pin, that statue was a carved crystal version of exactly the same image. They both even had the same slightly impish smile on their faces.

Smile? I hadn't noticed that in Dallas. My pin actually had a smile on his face. Certainly not as "fierce" as Clara had said.

"So, you're enjoying this, are you, Michael?" I said to the pin. Then I noticed that the desk clerk was now looking at me and smiling, too.

It was then that I decided that I had embarrassed myself enough in the lobby for one night, so I walked over to the French doors by the elevator and went out into the garden.

Chapter 6

When I was growing up, some of my favorite outings were to the Los Angeles County Arboretum. Since then I have always loved gardens, hiking paths, parks, or any place that lets me be surrounded by trees and other plants.

This courtyard was actually more like Shangri La than just a hotel garden. There was no apparent roof, but the temperature was almost tropical.

The foliage ranged from thirty-foot tall palm trees to hibiscus. There were banana trees only a few yards away from a cedar. There were even orchids, in full bloom, mixing their fragrance with that of jasmine and apple blossoms. The variety seemed impossible.

Winding throughout the garden were paths that were lit from sources hidden in the nearby foliage. They meandered around small hills, past waterfalls, and over musically babbling brooks, but all led to a central clearing. This was ringed with benches and had a most unusual centerpiece.

Rising maybe fifteen feet out of a circular pool was a boulder of granite with golden veins. It had three vertical faces, with water cascading over them into the pool below. Atop the boulder was some sort of fruit tree that I did not recognize.

I walked around this amazing fountain, viewing each of its almost identical faces, and quickly realized that I would enjoy spending a good deal of the next week in this spectacular garden.

As I finished my circuit of the pool, I noticed that the center of the courtyard was also the highest point. The water from this fountain flowed out of the pool in three streams, running under the walkway, and branching out to feed all of the brooks in the garden.

I was just turning to explore another path when I saw a tall gray-haired man in jeans, a light blue polo shirt, and cowboy boots, sitting on a bench watching me.

When our eyes met, he smiled, and I went over to meet him.

"This must be your first visit," he said, halfway chuckling, and stood up. "I could tell by the way your mouth is hanging open. I'm Gabe."

"Uh, hi. Yes, it is." I shook his hand and introduced myself.

"Well, your timing is good. Many of the Members will be here this week, and the garden is at its best. Just be thankful you got your invitation when you did."

"What invitation?" I said, confused.

His smile grew broader, if that was possible. "Oh, you were invited, or you wouldn't have found the place. Michael tells me that you have a guest membership, with all the privileges of being a full Member. You must have impressed somebody."

"Excuse me, but Michael who? Membership in what?" I blurted out; all of the day's surprises finally making my mind say 'TILT.' "I'm sorry, but today has been long and very strange. What are you talking about?"

In response he looked at me kindly and pointed at my jacket lapel.

"Michael, the Archangel. Your pin! That angel you're wearing tells me that you're a guest member. Whoever gave you that pin liked you enough to give you a gift, a complimentary first-class visit here, in Paradise. Well, as close to it as I've seen in a long time.

"They also knew that you were ready for it, even though you might not agree at first.

"Let me guess," He continued, "it was Clara who gave you the pin, wasn't it?"

"Yes, it was," I stammered, starting to feel a little bit foolish. "How did you know?"

"Oh, she is amazing. She is the best I know at spotting a diamond in the rough. She's sent quite a few guests to us, and she's never been wrong about their readiness.

"You'll see what I mean in the morning. That's when the fun begins and you'll get a chance to meet the other Members. This is their week to play, but I can guarantee you'll end up learning a lot from them."

"Who are these Members? Members in what?" I finally asked.

"Well, it's a very old club, shall we say. We try to help people and to pass on our knowledge to those who are ready." He tried to explain, obviously choosing his words carefully. "Clara must think you're good and ready."

"You mean this is some kind of cult? Is this your way of getting new members?" I asked, knowing somehow that that wasn't the case.

"Oh, no! You can't become a full Member," he said laughingly. "You're given this one visit. Then you'll have to leave, taking whatever truth you can accept with you. Anything you can't accept, you'll forget. If it turns out that you weren't ready for any of it, you'll forget the whole experience and your mind will come up with a nice safe story to cover the whole thing. Probably an alien abduction or something like that."

I was feeling a bit more at ease with all this, so I asked, "Okay, that's fair, but who are you people anyway?"

His reply almost made me go looking for my car. "We're angels!" he announced.

"Uh-huh! Angels? Okay!" I noticed that I was backing away, and forced my legs to stop.

"Don't act so surprised. You've always heard we existed. Why be so shocked when you finally meet one? Don't you believe in angels?"

I was beginning to feel like George Bailey in the movie, "It's A Wonderful Life." This led me to ask the obvious question. "Okay, Gabriel, so where's your wings?"

The last thing that I remember that evening was Gabe smiling, as he seemed to grow another foot taller and said, "I don't usually do this for just anyone, but...."

I watched as an enormous pair of radiant wings spread out from behind him, glowing with the pure white light of Love.

That's when I fainted.

Chapter 7

There was a tapping, like a fingernail tapping on glass. This was followed by a soothing chime, which was followed by the sound of someone pounding on wood.

I opened my eyes, and the light was blinding. "Gabe?" I asked, hazily remembering the last thing that I had seen.

No, this light was sunlight, and it was morning. I was in bed, a strange bed in a beautiful room of blue, white, and gold. My clothes were hung over the chair in the corner.

"It's real?" I wondered aloud, as the noises that had awakened me were repeated.

The first noise was a tapping, and a shadow, at my window. At a third floor window, I suddenly recalled.

The chime was coming from a telephone on the side table.

As I started to reach for that, I heard the pounding again on my room door. This was followed by the jingling of keys, and then rushing footsteps.

I picked up the phone and mumbled "Hello?" Thomas ran into the bedroom and straight toward the window.

"Oh excuse me, sir. I apologize for the disturbance," he hurriedly said to me as he threw open the window and began to lean out.

"Are you awake?" asked Gabe's deep voice on the other end of the phone.

"What? Uh, yes, good morning." I confusedly replied, looking in vain for an alarm clock to find out what time it was.

"Sir, you know the rules! Get back in here!" cried Thomas, apparently to someone outside my window. He was trying unsuccessfully to maintain decorum and still get cooperation. "Flying is allowed in the Aviary only. Now come back inside this instant."

"Sounds like you're having a party up there." Gabe said with a chuckle.

"I don't know what we're having up here." I bewilderedly responded.

"Get back in here, now!" demanded Thomas, trying to summon up a commanding tone and leaning further out of the window.

Just then, I saw the shadow move in front of the window. It then went straight up, taking poor Thomas with it, leaving behind a short "yelp" of indignation.

I ran to the window in time to hear Thomas' voice from high above yelling, "Oh, yes, very funny! Very funny indeed! Now put me down!"

"Are you still there?" asked Gabe from the receiver still clutched in my hand.

"Uh, yes. I think one of the Members was just outside my window. He seems to have abducted Thomas, the desk clerk." I tried to explain. "Thomas was upset about something."

"Oh, is that all?" Gabe seemed relieved. "Thomas is a stickler for the rules and thinks it's his job to enforce them. When they're here, the Members like things, shall we say, a bit less structured. So, Thomas gets less respect than he'd like."

"Some of the rules were made a long time ago and nobody remembers why. One such rule is the one about no flying except in the Aviary, above the garden.

"It's a dumb rule, but it's also one of Thomas' pet peeves. Since it seems to entertain everyone, including Thomas, we've never gotten around to changing it.

"Come on down and meet me for breakfast. We can talk and I'll show you around. Say, in forty-five minutes?"

"Okay, forty-five minutes." I said and hung up the phone.

It was then that I noticed the group of people, or whatever they were, just outside my door. It was still standing open, with Thomas' key ring hanging from the lock. The window was open and a cold breeze blew through, and into the hall, raising goose bumps on my bare skin.

"Excuse me," I said quickly, as I closed the door. I suddenly realized that, while I don't consider myself overly shy, I don't really enjoy being the only one naked, standing in front of a crowd; even a crowd of angels.

Before I showered, I tried to call my wife at her hotel in Utah, but only succeeded in leaving a message.

Needless to say, it was a message without much in the way of details. This was a story that would be hard to tell to another live person, much less trying to leave it as a phone message on a machine.

After a quick shower and shave, I dressed and went down to meet Gabe for breakfast. I didn't quite know what to expect from a day at a resort full of angels.

As I entered the restaurant, Gabe met me at the door and led me over to a table, where two other members were already seated.

"This is Anna and Celeste," he said, as I shook the hand of each.

I had already noticed that the only obvious difference between the Members and us common humans seemed to be their quiet air of calmness and confidence. Otherwise, Pinhead Butte Resort seemed like any other ritzy getaway, with people walking around in warm-up suits, tennis outfits, and jeans. Not a toga, flowing robe, or gossamer wing in sight.

Anna and Celeste were no exception.

Anna seemed to be in her mid-thirties, with light blonde hair, jeans and a "Hard Rock Cafe - London" sweatshirt.

Celeste looked a bit older, early forties, and was black. She wore a blue and gold warm-up suit that was the same design as I had seen many times in the J.C. Penney's catalog.

The breakfast buffet was as lavish as the one for dinner had been the night before, but I was still too keyed up to eat. So, over a glass of orange juice, I tried to get down to the business of finding out what was happening here, and why I had been brought into it.

I got right to the point, "Gabe, what is this all about? What is going on here?"

"I told you that last night, in the garden, don't you remember? Or did you crack your head on the walk when you passed out?"

He looked around; like he wanted to make sure nobody was listening, leaned over the table to me and whispered, quite seriously, "You don't want me to show you my wings again, in front of all of these people, do you?"

After a second, all three of them broke out laughing.

A few seconds later, I couldn't help but start laughing, too.

Here I was at a lavish resort, in breathtaking country, surrounded by Beings that could answer every question I ever had, and all I could do was doubt and whine! No, I could do more; I could also laugh.

I had never thought of angels laughing. I soon saw that most of the dining room was laughing with us, and their laughter sounded miraculous. The rest were just looking on and smiling, not knowing the joke, but enjoying the merriment.

Just as the laughter started to subside, Gabe pointed at me, then put his elbow on the table, with his arm and hand pointing straight up. After a second, he let his hand fall limply onto the table, in an obvious reference to my fainting in the garden, and the laughter started anew, ringing out into the hallways.

After a few minutes, the room started settling down again and Gabe was wiping tears from his eyes.

"My, you do keep things entertaining," Celeste commented to me. "I hear you had some excitement up in your room this morning, too.

Something about Albert trying to play with your head, by flying over to tap on your window."

"I hear he even took Thomas for a little ride," Anna cried giggling. "I wish I could've seen the look on Thomas' face. He must have been furious!"

"Well, you should have seen the look on Mortal Boy here, when he realized that Thomas left the door wide open, with him standing there in his birthday suit drawing a crowd of admirers. Just standing there with the phone in his ear," Celeste finished, holding up an invisible telephone.

Gabe tried to keep a straight face, but, seeing how embarrassed I was getting; he finally gave up and burst out laughing again.

When I gave in to the chuckles too, Gabe walked around the table, slapped me on the shoulder, and said, "You're all right. You'll fit in just fine. Let's go for a walk."

Chapter 8

Gabe escorted me out of San Miguel's and through the lobby.

When we came to the edge of the conversation pit and I saw that it was full of people, it struck me that there were no children. I hadn't seen even one of the cute little cherubs that you see in paintings. Then I remembered the little girl, Linda, from the night before.

"Gabe, I have a question," I began, stopping in front of the statue of Michael. "Last night I met some people over there by the pool. One was a little girl and the others seemed to be her parents. Were they angels too?"

Gabe smiled. "I wondered when you'd ask about them. No, they were humans and were here to meet you."

"What do you mean, to meet me? As soon as we met, they rushed off. Who were they?"

"Who did they say they were?" The question sounded like Gabe was playing the role of psychoanalyst.

"The parents were Gene and Alameda, and the girl was... No, wait just a minute,,," I stammered.

My wife's mother and her family used to call her "Tootsie." Gene and Alameda were her parents' names.

"How can that be?" I continued. "That little girl was all of three and my wife's parents passed away years ago. Her father died when she was little."

"Face it, angels know things that you don't," Gabe explained, starting my first lesson on the true nature of the universe. "No, that's not right. Angels *remember* things that you don't."

"Angels see time and space, and all of the other dimensions, in the same way that the Creator does. All of the dimensions are there, of course, but they don't matter a whole heck of a lot.

"To an angel, time isn't linear and neither is space. We can be anywhere, or anywhen, just by deciding to be there and then. We can even project mortals to a time and place where they're needed, without disturbing the linear existence that they see as their lives."

I was awestruck! "You mean that actually was my wife and her parents here last night?"

"That was her. When you talk to her, describe the statue and she'll have a vague memory of a dream from long ago. Nothing detailed, just a pretty angel and a nice old man... you." He grinned.

"But why did you bring them here?"

"Just a little object lesson for you, my friend. I thought you'd get it last night, but at least you did catch the connection between your pin and the statue. That way we were able to get around to the fainting part a little bit sooner."

"Actually," he continued, "you took the whole revelation deal pretty well. I had one guy who ran through one of the French doors; it scared him so much. But, like I told you last night, you aren't invited until you're ready to handle it. After he settled down, he did just fine.

"As for your wife, she and her parents were here as examples of the irrelevance of time and space. They were here last night in your reality, but she experienced it when she was three and in California. Go figure!"

He turned and headed for the elevator with me following.

We rode to the third floor in silence, then crossed the hall, and took the spiral stairway up into the observation tower.

The tower consisted of a circular room that sat neatly atop of, and covering, the entire corner of the resort building. It had a domed roof that was held up by twelve marble columns ranged around the edge of the circle. Between the columns were banisters that were also made of finely carved marble.

From the back of this rooftop perch, you could see straight down into the garden and, from the front, out over the vast lawn and into the valley beyond. In any direction you looked, however, you could enjoy the beauty of the mountains and forest as they rolled off into the distance.

"So, why do you come here?" I finally asked. "In all of creation, why here and now? Why the private resort?"

"Oh, it's just a remote spot, one of many, where we can go to relax. We all keep pretty busy and sometimes we just need to go somewhere to unwind. Oddly enough, mortals aren't the only ones who need to let their hair down now and then.

"Like them," he said, indicating a group playing some sort of game out on the lawn. "They all spend most of their time as guides and guardian angels. Most of them have been watching over people who are fighting some kind of religious war for generations.

"Both sides in that war are constantly praying to their god, a god who both sides call by the same name, to smite the other side. Well, these angels are supposed to help answer prayers, but not like that. What's a Creator-loving angel supposed to do?

"They do what they have to do," he said, showing a somber side now. "They save as many as they can. They whisper words of wisdom to those who'll listen. And they weep for all the rest.

"And every now and then," he added, smiling as he gazed out over the lawn, "they step out of that place and time and come to a different here and now. They know that they will go back, picking up right where and when they left off, to save, and whisper, and weep. But now, like I told you last night, they are here to play. And so am I. And so are you."

"To play?" I asked. "I thought I was here to learn."

"Well, of course!" he exclaimed. "Don't children learn by playing? Aren't lessons easier to learn if they're fun? Aren't you always telling people 'if you're not learning, you're not living'?"

"Well then, let's go join the game." And we were suddenly standing in the middle of the lawn.

Chapter 9

"What the…" I caught myself before finishing the often used phrase. When I turned to ask Gabe how we got there, I saw only his back as he ran off across the lawn.

I found myself in the midst of a mass of bodies, all of them involved in a game that seemed to be a strange version of soccer.

Why was it strange? Well, for one thing, there didn't seem to be any separation of players into teams, like the soccer that I am used to. It was more of a free-for-all, with one player passing the ball to another at one moment and then stealing it from him soon after.

There were no goal lines either, just sort of a flowing tide of players moving this direction and that, seemingly at random. In fact, goals would have been made nearly impossible, since the game was actually taking place in three dimensions.

In apparent total disregard for the house rules, Thomas' feelings, and all of the known laws of physics, the field of play included the area many yards above the lawn, as well as below it.

At one point, I saw what would have otherwise been considered an absolutely normal lateral pass, but executed from a banking turn at about 100 feet above the ground.

This was followed by a charge downfield (with the own part being literal) straight into the sod, with the entire mob following close behind.

The lawn was quiet for about three minutes, except for muffled shouts from under foot. Then the whole group burst back into the air, this time chasing Gabe. I found out later that he had taken the ball by hiding behind a boulder and pouncing on it by surprise.

No, this wasn't a game that I was able to join, but it certainly drove home that fact that I was in the midst of some interesting company.

After about an hour, the players began to lose interest in the game and started wandering off of the field and back to the lodge.

When Gabe finally dropped out, he came back over to me with a puzzled look.

"Why didn't you get in the game?" he asked, as we walked back to the lobby steps. "Don't you like soccer?"

"Sure, but it's been a long time," I replied, trying to be cool. "Besides, I left my winged cleats at home."

"Okay, smart-aleck, but you didn't even try. Even if you choose to remember only the limitations in your life, you could have gone after the ball when it was on your two dimensional playing field. Instead you just watched."

"Why are you so disappointed?" I asked Gabe, a bit irked by his apparent judgment of me. "Was this another test, another object lesson? Was I supposed to jump into the game and become so involved that I just started following the pack up into the air or under the ground?"

"Something like that," he calmly replied. "It wasn't a planned test, just a little diversion that we all enjoy. But, yes, I did hope that you'd get involved enough that you'd let your subconscious mind remember what you're capable of.

"Don't you see? This matter you perceive as reality isn't real at all. It's illusion, it's an image, it's…it's like what you see on a movie screen, a projection, but in more than two dimensions."

"What you saw today was just us ignoring the dimensions of the screen and playing out into the theater. If you want to get right down to it, the reason people don't normally see angels at all, is because they expect to see us within the limits of the screen, instead of noticing that there's one in the next seat, offering to share popcorn."

"What has popcorn got to do with it?" I asked, knowing that I had somehow missed the point.

"Oh, well," he sighed, as we entered the lobby, ignoring the look of disgust he got from Thomas when he brushed the dirt from his shoulder and onto the highly polished marble floor. "I had hoped for a little spontaneous remembering from you today. I guess we'll just have to go the long way around."

Brushing more dirt out of his hair, he continued, "Why don't you go explore and mingle for a while. I need to go clean up. Besides, there are others around who can contribute to your education, too.

"Let's meet for dinner later," he suggested, entering the elevator.

"Okay, what time and where?"

"When we get there," he replied, as the door started to close. "Time and space are irrelevant. Remember?"

Left on my own, I decided to walk all of the way around the first floor, to see if anything interesting was happening. Still not having signs to guide me, except in the restaurant, I found myself having to guess at what some of the rooms were for.

The gift shop was easy. They had a stock of every type of candy bar ever made. There was a rack of magazines, all of the special interest variety, but none of the major news types. There was even a jewelry section, which prominently displayed a collection of pins identical to the one that I wore.

Next to that were a clothing store, what appeared to be a beauty salon, and a video game parlor.

The latter was packed, with every machine in use and plenty of customers waiting their turns. Here were angels, standing in line to play the very same games that I had always thought of as a waste of time and money.

This surprised me. I would have thought that angels would find something better to do with their time.

Time? Oh, yeah, that was "irrelevant." I decided that, if you are immortal and have free access to any point in time that you like, you can do anything you like, whenever you like.

A little further down the hall I came to a storefront that didn't need a sign, even though it actually did have one.

"Now Showing" it said in dark blue letters on a gold background. This was the banner at the top of an empty movie poster frame. It hung on the wall in front of what was obviously the "small theater" that Lawrence had mentioned. Above the entrance there was also a standard white marquee, which was also blank.

The glass front door stood invitingly open, and the rich smell of fresh popcorn wafted out into the hallway. It was the most effective "OPEN" sign I'd ever encountered.

"Well," I told myself, "if angels can play video games with their non-relevant time, then I can create some time for a movie, even if I don't know what the movie will be."

Chapter 10

Pinhead Butte's "small theater" was far from small. Its 450 seat auditorium was enormous compared to some shopping mall theaters that I've seen. My guess was that it was built to hold all of the guests and most of the staff in comfort. It was designed to be able to show movies, or for live performances.

The only thing that was little about it was the lobby. This consisted of a relatively small entryway with restroom doors on each end and three sets of double doors leading into the auditorium, equally spaced along the wall. There was no actual concession stand, just a table with a soda dispenser, ice bucket, and cups, next to a small popcorn-vending cart.

After being lured in by the aroma of freshly popped popcorn, I was very disappointed to find that the holding area of the cart was now empty except for a few crumbs.

I considered making another batch, but didn't see a supply of raw materials anywhere in sight. And so, popcornless, I went into the auditorium to see what kind of movies angels watch.

I was slightly surprised to find what I recognized as a fairly recent release, "The Preacher's Wife," showing on the screen. I'm not sure what I'd expected; maybe "The Ten Commandments" or something equally biblical. But I could also see how they could relate to this one, too. In fact, the house was nearly full.

The movie was about half over, so I found an aisle seat near the back, trying not to disturb anyone. I had seen this movie before and I only needed a moment to catch on to where they were in the story.

Just as I was really settling in and getting "into" the movie, I heard a noise from beside me. Sort of a "pssst", like someone trying to get someone else's attention.

Annoyed by the interruption, I looked down the row and saw a man in a suit and a slightly floppy hat, looking at me from two seats away.

"Do you want some of my popcorn?" he whispered.

"No, thank you," I said, turning back to the screen.

He got up and moved to the seat next to me. "Are you sure? I noticed you didn't have any and, after all, what's a movie without popcorn? I remember when I first saw…"

"If you don't mind, I'm trying to watch…", I started to interrupt him. But then, I turned my head and got a good look at him.

"Clarence?" I gasped. He was the spitting image of the character that Henry Travers played in "It's A Wonderful Life." He was even wearing the same outfit, and funny looking hat.

"I thought you were just a character in a movie!" I managed to continue.

"Oh, my, no," he stammered. "I'm as real as you are." He poked me in the shoulder with his finger. "And you seem pretty real to me."

Those in the seats around us were now turning and giving us completely non-angelic looks, so Clarence suggested that we talk outside.

"You see," he continued when we were back out in the hallway, "you thought of me as just a character. You believe that after the movie is shot, and the actors leave the set, all of the characters they portrayed cease to exist.

"That just isn't true. Some of the characters that are created in art are actually echoes of beings that exist, or existed, in other places and times. Some even resemble beings that exist outside of the dimensions that you perceive. Like, angels.

"Oh, I was flattered by the character in the movie, in many ways, but I really prefer Sir Arthur Conan Doyle to Mark Twain, I don't wear underwear from the 1700's, I was never incarnate as a human, and I've always had my wings, thank you very much."

"But how did they get you down as good as they did?" I finally asked.

"You've heard the phrase 'Life Imitates Art'?" he asked.

"Well, that isn't very true either. Art really imitates truth, although it's by no means limited to it.

"When I said that some characters were echoes, what I meant is that the imagination of a mortal is sometimes inspired by things that they sense around them, or things that they subconsciously remember. Other things, like vampires, ghosts, and demons are entirely creations of artists' strange imaginings, and the Creator only knows where those come from!"

"I was interested in that movie from the day they started to write it. In fact, I spent a lot of time watching over them as they wrote the screenplay and did the casting. You can imagine my surprise when Henry Travers got the part of an angel named Clarence, and he ended up performing it in a way that looked and sounded a lot like me.

"I knew that we could inspire people's thoughts and actions, but to have them sense my presence that strongly really amazed me."

"So you sort of hung around the studio and just watched?" I wondered out loud. "You didn't appear to any of them, or anything like that?"

"Well, no, I don't think so," he said, thinking it over again. "No, I didn't."

"Mortals live in their limited world," he continued, "even though they- you are able to sense much more.

Those who open themselves up to this ability are called 'psychics', or 'mediums', or 'gifted'; when, actually they are still using only a small portion of their potential.

"In fact, you have more in common with the angels than you think." He smiled. "It's just that you don't remember who you are and what you're capable of."

"Why do you and Gabe say things like that?" I was getting defensive. "What is there to remember? I thought I was here to learn, not to be reminded of something I already know."

"If you remembered your true nature, your true source, you'd know who you really are. You wouldn't need us to keep trying to remind you."

He was beginning to get me riled, saying things that didn't answer questions, things that seemed more like riddles. "Look, I know who I am!" I was even starting to sound like George Bailey, "and my memory is just fine."

"No, you don't remember who you are," he said in a calm, firm voice. "But you will, sonny, before the week is out." He then turned and walked back into the theater.

I decided not to catch the rest of the movie. Instead, I made my way out into the garden to sit and think.

Chapter 11

Since I had covered about a quarter of the distance around the first floor before entering the theater, I found myself in a different part of the garden than I had visited the night before. It was just as marvelous, but filled with an entirely different variety of plants.

Another difference from the previous evening was that there were now others walking along the paths, alone, in pairs, or sitting on the benches.

It seems that angels need quiet time in beautiful surroundings just as much as we "mortals" do.

"Mortals." I wasn't sure that I liked that term. Sure these characters were angels, but did they have to use a term like that to separate us from them? Since the word refers to those who die, was our having a physical life span that important? Wasn't that a bit elitist?

After all, I was their guest here. Wouldn't "humans" be a more polite term?

I was just considering how to bring this up with Gabe, when something red fell out of the sky right in front of me, and burst, soaking my shoes and pant legs with water.

A water balloon? From where?

I started to look for someone in the garden who might have tossed it at me, but there was no one that close. I was also too far from the wall of the building for it to have been dropped from a room window.

I was just starting to look up, when a stream of water, from above and behind me, soaked my head and back. This was followed by an outburst of laughter, also from above me.

I turned and looked up to see a half dozen angels, wings unfurled, armed with Super Soakers and water balloons. Among them were Celeste and Anna.

"Hey, Mortal Boy," Celeste called from about twenty feet above. "You're sure hard to hit when you're moving!"

I looked back down the trail and saw that it was littered with balloon fragments and dotted with puddles of water all the way back as far as I could see.

"You just need more target practice." I said, smiling up at them.

"Come on up and join us," Anna said, bouncing a blue balloon in her hand, "there's lots of juicy targets down there today."

I was about to make some lame comment about borrowing a set of wings, when Thomas came running down the path shouting, "Now stop that. Stop that right now!"

Celeste looked at Anna with an impish grin. Then she and the others moved to form a circle above him.

I knew what was coming, but he didn't seem to.

A moment later, they were all flying off toward the center of the garden, presumably to refill their water guns at the fountain, and Thomas was standing there drenched to the skin.

"Well, that was fun!" he said hotly, apparently to nobody in particular, but looking up to the sky, as if for guidance.

Noticing me, and the fact that I was also somewhat wet, he turned back into the prim and proper butler-type that he was before.

"Oh, I am sorry about this, sir. I will send for a towel for you immediately," he blustered, apparently forgetting that he needed one far more than I did.

"That bunch does this every time they come here," he continued, "but what can one do?"

"So is this their way of initiating mortals?" I asked.

"Oh, no, sir! They've been soaking anyone in the garden who seemed too serious. They don't care, angel or not. If you're down, or just deep in thought, you're another target to them. They're really only trying to help keep everyone in the here and now."

"What do you mean, Thomas?"

"Angels come here for their own good. You know, for vacation, outside of the time and place that they're working in," he replied.

"That's what Gabe told me, too. But I still have trouble with the concept of angels needing vacations."

"Oh, they certainly do, sir," he said, as if it should have been obvious. "Angels remember everything. They were there when time began, and they know our true nature."

"They also see all of our pain and stupidity. Do you enjoy visiting sick people in the hospital?"

"Who does?" I answered, surprised at the question.

"They do. Partly because they are trying to help ease the pain, but mostly because they love us. Even though we fight with each other and bring all of our trouble on ourselves, they still care enough to help."

"In fact, it's just that caring that creates the need for this place, and others like it. How long do you think they can go on, knowing what they do about us, watching what we do to ourselves, and still remain sane?"

"That blessed group," he said, pointing after our angelic bombardiers, "helps to keep things light. They help keep the visiting members' minds off of the pain of their jobs."

I couldn't believe the tone of his voice. Was it deep respect, or was it awe?

"But they treat you with so little respect," I began.

"No, no, that's not true," he interrupted with a grin. "My behavior encourages the way they respond. I'm the officious clown as a distraction.

My job here is to give them something else to think about. They know that and they play along."

"But what about when I arrived," I asked, "was that part of the act too? Why did you act that way with me?"

"No, that wasn't an act," he chuckled. "I hadn't seen your pin, so I was being obnoxious to get you to leave. Simon and I were surprised to see you when you came in. Non-angels normally can't find Pinhead Buttes unless they are invited, and we hadn't been told to expect any guests this week. We just assumed that you were lost and somehow stumbled upon us."

"So, you guys, the staff, you're all normal humans, right?"

"Well, yes, pretty much," he replied, trying to phrase his answer carefully.

"What do you mean 'pretty much'?"

"We've all worked here for a long time. In fact, I've been here since the Pinhead Buttes Resort was created. That was about 75 years ago, earth time."

"But…" I started to protest.

"Yes, I know, I look about 35," he explained. "That's because this place is actually located just outside of normal space and time. We all experience the passage of time, but not earth time, just relative time."

"If I were to leave here, as I have done for short periods in the past, I would return to normal time and age normally while I was gone. While I'm here, however, earth time has no effect."

"In fact, our relative time doesn't even parallel earth time. For example, the lady who was our guest last week, in our relative time, came from an earth date in 2034."

"Speaking of time," Gabe's voice came from behind me, "I think it's dinner time."

"Right you are, sir," said Thomas, turning to slosh his way back to the building.

Gabe noticed the water oozing out of Thomas' shoes and said, "Uh, Thomas?"

Thomas stopped and turned around, but before he could say anything in reply, realized that he was suddenly completely dry.

"Thank you, sir," he said to Gabe. And then to me, as he left, "See what I mean?"

"I see you experienced the 'Blue Birds' jokingly call themselves. Spreading happiness in their own inimitable way." Gabe chuckled. "Sorry you got hit before I could warn you."

"No problem. It was refreshing." I said, suddenly realizing that they had actually brightened my mood.

"Yeah, right, refreshing." He didn't sound convinced. "Ready for dinner?"

Chapter 12

Dinner that evening was more subdued than breakfast had been. Gabe and I ate together, but we didn't talk much and we weren't joined by any of the others.

Of course, after not eating at breakfast and having ignored lunch completely, I was a bit on the hungry side and took full advantage of the buffet.

Finally, we went back out into the garden, to the place where I had met Gabe the night before.

As we sat down on the bench, he asked, "So do feel you learned anything today?"

"I suppose so," I replied. "Mostly I learned a little about the nature of angels, that you're a lot more playful than I believed before. I mean, laughter and games and practical jokes.

"I'm still a little damp from the attack of the 'Blue Birds of Happiness'."

"I was always led to believe that you spent your days singing in some great celestial choir, or saving us from breaking our necks doing something foolish."

"What else have you learned about us?" Gabe prompted.

"You have enough job stress and disappointments that you need to get away from it all now and then. That you do this by stepping out of time and space and coming to places like this. And that you like video games, soccer, and movies.

"How's that, coach?" I concluded.

"Not bad, for a start. What does all that tell you about us, though?" He was prodding me now, trying to get me to come to some conclusion.

I really didn't see where he was going with this, so I flippantly said, "I guess we're not all that different after all, are we?"

He let out a great sigh of relief. "Very good! You remembered."

"What? Remembered what? I was just kidding."

"No, you weren't just kidding. That was your inner self expressing the truth you have always known, but didn't remember. Humans and angels are really only different in a few rather unimportant, ways."

"First, and most important," he explained, "humans don't remember their true nature. Oh, you know it, deep down inside, and you spend most of your lives trying to find that truth. Even though you don't know what you're looking for, you know that it will give you peace, and explain why you're here, and what you're supposed to be doing.

"The other is the physical body thing. Even in your selfimposed amnesia about yourself, you still remember that there is something of the spirit in you. This, too, causes you to seek for truth, although your physical senses seem to indicate that you cease to exist when your body dies."

"Okay, then, how are we alike?" I barked. I was upset, without really knowing why. He wasn't saying anything that was new to me, but I felt myself resisting it.

"In just about every other way," he said, smiling.

"For instance?"

For now, let's just say that the one you call God created all spirits, including angels and humans, at once and exactly the same. We're all made of the same eternal, pan-dimensional stuff. We have no real limits that I know of.

"The only limits that any of the Creator's creatures have are those that are imposed by its own consciousness. Humans are born with a mental block that causes them to forget some really important things. Then they spend their lives creating versions of the missing bits that will fit their circumstances, and still not make them uncomfortable.

"The fact is, some of the belief systems that humans have come up with are pretty amazing. Not quite as good as the truth, but very believable."

I was shocked. "Do you mean that all of the religions that humans have believed in, and sacrificed for, and been martyred for, are false? That it's all been a waste of time?"

"No, not at all," he said soothingly. "Actually, in some ways, they were all right. No one faith has the whole answer, but since you all knew the truth subconsciously, you brought at least some of it into each of your different religions.

"We'll get into the really good reason for what some philosophers have called the 'veil of forgetfulness' later, but for now, let's just say that humans have done very well with the little bit of information they've had to work with.

"Angels, on the other hand, aren't burdened with the 'veil'! No, we can do miracles, travel in and out of time and space, and so much more, just because we remember that we aren't limited.

"Humans can do the same things, all of them. All you have to do is remember who you are. The capabilities are just the benefits of knowing your true self.

"Look, you've been given a lot to think about today," he concluded. "Why don't you go get some rest? Meet me up in the tower in the morning and I'll try to help you remember. Okay?"

"Alright, what time?" I asked out of habit, but I already knew what his answer would be.

He smiled roguishly, pointed at me, and said, "You'll know." He then walked off into the garden.

I went back up to my room, and called my wife.

She was doing fine, and wanted to know everything that was happening. Not being sure myself, I tried to make it all sound as normal as possible, which left very little to talk about.

After we hung up, I decided to take Gabe's advice and turn in.

That night I had some very vivid dreams. Dreams of flying with the 'Blue Birds' in the aviary, of visiting other places and times, and one about a strange world where everybody had the same face.

In this last dream, I could sense the individuals and knew who they were. But they all had the same radiant face. They all glowed with the same light that I had seen when Gabe had spread his wings the night before, the soothing pure white light of Love.

I woke before dawn, and quickly dressed. Being up this early, I wanted to see the sunrise from the observation tower.

When I reached the top of the stairs, I saw that the sky was just getting light in the east and the show was about to begin.

Chapter 13

As the eastern sky began to lighten, it silhouetted the mountains on each side of a v-shaped pass, creating a natural, and thoroughly impressive, frame for the upcoming light show.

Some sunrises and sunsets are nice, but nothing special. Either there are too many, or not enough, clouds. Sometimes the magic just doesn't seem to be there.

This was not going to be one of those.

Instead, as the sky brightened, I could see that clouds had formed above the horizon in just the right quantity and position to create that awe-inspiring ray effect sunrises are famous for. As for color, the sky was already painted with assorted shades of crimson and orange and gold a full ten minutes before the sun even made its appearance.

I was standing there, mouth agape, watching what was probably the most beautiful display of natural wonder I had seen in my life, when I became aware of sound. It was very faint at first, but rapidly increased in volume, until it seemed to vibrate my very soul.

It was the sound of the Celestial Choir, singing notes, not words, to accompany the miracle that was taking place off to the east.

At first I could not see where the music came from, but as the volume rose, I saw a glow that came from down in the courtyard, from the area of the garden's central fountain. As the sky continued to brightened, and the volume of the choir increased, this glow also increased until it was a brilliant white ring, encircling the fountain.

The music continued, and the ring of light rose until it was level with the roof of the lodge. A ring of pure white light hovered in the air maybe fifty yards in front of me.

As my eyes became more accustomed to the brilliance, I was finally able to make out the individual forms of perhaps three dozen angels, their wings moving slowly, holding hands to form the ring. The light was obviously from the same source as I had seen when Gabe had displayed his wings to me on the first night.

"Another perfect day, but then again, they all are, aren't they?"

The voice came unexpectedly from behind me, causing me to jump. I spun around to see Gabe sitting on the railing, his wings spread and shining brightly.

"Enjoying the show?" he asked as his wings folded and disappeared behind him.

"Not bad," I said, forcing myself to sound unimpressed. "Do you always make this kind of a production number out of it?"

He grinned and pointed behind me, out over the courtyard. "No, just when our guests make the effort to get up in time to see it."

I turned and looked where the angelic chorus had been hovering a minute before. They were still there, but now they all had their wings pointed straight out from their shoulders, tips overlapping. They were in two parallel lines, one above the other, facing me.

When they knew that I was looking, they began singing the song "One," from "A Chorus Line," and performed a Rockettes-like kick dance. After one verse, they all bowed in unison and then, laughing, broke formation, flying off in various directions.

I heard Gabe begin to chuckle behind me.

"Cute," I said, turning to face him again. "Real cute."

"We thought you might like that. Want to see it again?"

"See it again?" I wondered out loud.

"Sure!" he beamed. "Remember what you learned about time and space? Well, if time and space are something you can step out of, why can't you move around in them? Watch this."

I turned back to the courtyard to see the angelic chorus lines reform, do their little dance routine, rearrange themselves into the luminous ring, and finally settle back into the center of the garden. All the while, their voices could be heard, as beautiful as before, but with that strange backward sound you get when playing a record the wrong way.

Everything stopped for a second, and then began again, at the same point where I had arrived at the tower.

"This time, listen to the notes, but watch the sunrise," Gabe instructed.

A strange effect was immediately noticeable. The shades and patterns of color in the sunrise seemed to shift and change with the tones that the choir was singing.

Suddenly, everything stopped, as if someone had hit a great cosmic pause button.

"Do you see them?" Gabe asked. "Do you see the tonal patterns?"

"Yes, what is that?"

"Everything is made of pure energy. Not just light and sound and radio waves and such, but matter too. And being energy, everything has a vibrational frequency. You do, I do, the earth does, and so does the sun.

"Now, this vibration is unique to each thing in creation and manifests itself in the look, feel, sound, smell, and taste of the object.

"As everything emits vibrations, the fields of wave patterns interact, creating harmonies and interference patterns, like the ripple patterns do when you drop two stones into a pond.

"The truth is, how you feel about someone, or something, has more to do with how your inner being senses the interplay of your energy frequencies, than how good or bad they smell, or what brand of clothing they wear.

"Getting back to the tonal patterns, what you just saw was an example of how two different manifestations of the same energy, one in the form of sunlight, and the other as sound from our friends out there, can form interference patterns and create a new set of vibrations."

The show then resumed, a myriad of colors and patterns flowing across the eastern sky.

This time, when it concluded, the choir formed their two ranks and Gabe and I applauded them. After a couple of seconds, they bowed, broke formation, and dispersed.

One flew over and landed on the deck of the tower. It was Clarence.

"Well," he began, "second day, and you're deep into vibrational patterns. Good for you! Gabe'll have you flying soon."

"Flying?" I gasped, looking at how far it was down into the garden. "I'm not an angel. I don't have any wings. How am I supposed to fly?"

Clarence chuckled, "Since you're so fond of movies, try this line: 'Wings? You don't need no stinking wings!'" This last he said in a thick Mexican accent.

"Clarence," Gabe interrupted, "I don't think he's ready to solo yet. We have a ways to go before flight training."

"Okay," Clarence said, starting to lift off of the deck. Then, sailing smoothly out over the garden, he told me, "But I'll be waiting to hear a bell ring."

"Flying?" I said in disbelief, turning back to Gabe.

He walked over and put one hand on my shoulder.

"Don't think about that now," he said, seriously. "I promise I won't push you off of the roof." He paused. "At least, not until I'm sure nobody is standing where you might fall on them." He started to laugh.

Chapter 14

After going back to my room to shower, I had breakfast with Gabe. Without really discussing it, we had gotten into a habit of having meals together, but not discussing any of the lessons while we ate.

After breakfast, we went into the lobby and sat in the conversation pit, next to the crystal statue of Michael. As soon as we were comfortable, Gabe began the day's lesson.

"What do you think is the difference between you and I?"

"That question is either very easy," I started, "or very deep.

"The easy answer is that you're an angel and I'm a human. The deeper answer would have to get into the nature of angels and humans and…"

"No," he interrupted, "the difference between us is vibration."

"That's all?" I stammered. "What about the stories of the creation and the legends about angels and their power? Aren't angels special, holier than humans?"

"Angels are creatures of energy, but so are humans," he explained. "Holiness is a human concept to explain supernatural powers that appear to come from God.

"Supernatural is really just another way of saying superhuman. Anything that the majority of humans can't see themselves doing is automatically viewed as supernatural.

"In reality, someone who displays the characteristics of 'holiness' is just someone who's more open to their true nature. They're not as limited by the 'veil of forgetfulness' as most other humans."

I had to ask, "So humans can do anything that angels can do, is that what you're saying?"

"More than that, I am saying that you and I are exactly the same. The only difference is that you're experiencing linear time while in a physical form. Other than that, we're just separate expressions of the same energy, with different vibrational frequencies and patterns.

"In fact, aside from vibration, we're exactly the same as everything else in creation."

"Is vibration what gives us different natures, different personalities?" I asked.

"It's what gives us different appearances, different features, everything that differentiates one creature from another.

"The interesting offshoot is that, if you want to really understand reality from the perspective of another, you just have to change your vibration to match theirs. Then you basically become them."

I must have looked as skeptical as I felt.

He got up. "Let's go for a walk and I'll help you see what I mean."

As we headed for the lobby door he continued, "Did you ever wonder why twenty people, all seeing exactly the same incident, describe what seems to be totally different scenes?"

"Different perspectives?" I offered.

"Right! But how come they're all so different?"

"Different backgrounds? Different levels of color vision? Different levels of eyesight?" I was guessing.

"You weren't listening back there, were you?" he frowned. "No, what you perceive around you is based on how your vibrational frequency interacts with those around you.

"Remember the patterns and colors you saw this morning? Those were caused by the interaction of the wave patterns of the sunlight with the sound vibrations of the choir. What you saw was also different from what I did, however, because what you saw also was affected by your vibrational pattern."

"To someone else that view might have been bland and boring. It all depends on the interaction of their vibrational frequencies.

"That's also the truth in the old saying 'Beauty is in he eye of the beholder'.

"Beauty, or repulsiveness, is purely how we feel about the patterns created when our vibration interacts with someone else's vibration."

By now we were out on the lawn, walking toward the woods that bordered it.

"The day you arrived, you saw a herd of deer on your way up, right?" He paused, but not long enough for me to reply. "You watched each other for a while, but they never ran off, not seeming to be afraid of you."

I shouldn't have been surprised, but I was. "Yes, how did you know?"

"They weren't afraid because animals are incredibly attuned to the vibrations of others. They have to be. Those deer could feel that you weren't a threat. They knew your intent.

"There's a lot of truth in the old saying that a dog can sense fear. That's because the patterns that form during the interaction of two vibrations are the same for both creatures in the interaction. This pattern includes subtle messages about each one's intent and response to the interaction. Thus the dog will sense your fear, and the deer will sense your love.

"Okay," he continued, "based on all of this, how do you think you might be able to experience the exact point of view of another creature?"

"I suppose," I started slowly, "I would have to become that creature."

"Right!" he said, apparently having happily decided I wasn't irretrievably slow after all. "But how do you become that other creature?"

"From what you said, I suppose I would have to have the exact same vibrational pattern and frequency."

"Excellent!" he shouted. "What do you want to be first?"

"What?" I gasped, "I thought you were talking about theory. Now you want to turn me into a frog?"

He smiled. "A frog? No, too far up the food chain for the first time. Besides, you probably would have problems with eating flies, especially this soon after breakfast."

"How about a tree?" he said thoughtfully.

"But how..." I began.

Suddenly, I felt a change come over me. I was no longer myself, I was a tree.

I could feel my branches reaching up into the air and the cool breeze moving my leaves. On each individual leaf, I could feel the warmth of the sun and the energy that it brought. I felt the cool earth around my roots and the moisture that fed me from deep down in the soil.

I sensed the life around me everywhere. The bugs and worms that lived in the soil at my base, and the bird whose nest was neatly placed in the fork of one of my uppermost branches. I even felt the vibration of the earth itself, supportive and giving, the source of my life.

I began to experience even more vibrations of life around me. A squirrel as it jumped from one of my neighbor trees to another. A bug that nibbled delicately at one of my leaves. A Being of immense peace that stood by my trunk looking at me lovingly.

I knew that all was well, and I felt peace.

And then, I was my human self again, standing next to Gabe.

"Whoa!" I said, catching my balance. "How did you do that?"

"Simple," he said. "I varied my vibration in a way that it tuned yours to be that of a tree. How was it?"

"Amazing! I really felt like I was a tree."

"That's because you really were a tree." He chuckled gleefully. "It's like I told you, by changing your vibrational frequency and pattern, you change what you are!"

"Could I do that myself?" I was really getting excited.

"Wait a minute." He sounded cautious. "First off, yes, you can, but it takes a lot of practice, and you have to be careful."

"You might try to be an elephant and turn yourself into a trout, if you get the vibration wrong. You also have to pick things you wouldn't mind ending up as.

"The funny thing about actually experiencing the perspective of a different creature is that you might not want to, or remember how to, change back. You have to keep that in mind when you're trying to do this alone."

I thought about that, but was hooked. "I see what you mean. How do I change my vibration myself?"

"It really is easy," he said, almost reluctantly, "it just takes time and practice to master it. First, you have to learn to recognize your own vibration. This involves finding ways to isolate yourself from other vibrations and to extend your perceptions to pick it up.

"Next you have to do the same thing with the vibration of the creature you want to become. This means finding it's true vibration, not the interference pattern created by the interaction with yours."

"Sounds like a lot of work," I said, discouraged.

"Give it time, and if you want it bad enough, you'll do it," he consoled. "What do you want to be next?"

The rest of the day was like a dream. I was a robin, high up in the nest in the tree that I had been earlier. I was the deer that I had exchanged stares with two days earlier. I was a boulder that had sat there, undisturbed, for thousands of years.

Gabe helped me to become a dozen things. While I was each of them, I truly knew the world from their point of view and, amazingly, I even had their memories.

Yes, memories. The tree, the robin, and even the stone all have memories of their own existences.

By the time we returned to the lodge, I was exhausted, but I'd never felt so in touch with the world around me.

I was quiet through dinner and afterward, as we walked into the garden, Gabe asked if I was all right.

"Sure," I replied. "I was just trying to grasp it all. Having been all the things that I was today, I still can't say that I really understand the reason for it all.

"I mean, why are we here? Why does one creature have to nourish itself on another? What does it all mean?"

"You're not ready for all of that tonight," he tried to explain, "but there is a reason. Let's just say that it all works for the common good. Before the week is out, you'll understand it a lot better, but for now you just need to accept that the final reason is Love."

"Love?" I asked, "not 'God's Will' or something like that?"

He smiled. "'God's Will' is a good way to look at it. The Creator's plan is at work here, and this is all part of it."

I finally had the nerve to ask the big questions. "Really? So, who is this Creator? Is it Yahweh, or Allah, or whoever? Who do you work for? Which faith is the right one?"

"They all are," he said calmly. "I thought you knew that."

"Humans created all of the different religions to explain their different perceptions of the world around themselves. From the stone-age monkey worshipper to the televangelist, they've all created God in their own image."

"The Creator made it all, for its own reasons, but no creature is above another. The white human isn't better than the black, the human is no higher than the amoeba, and animals aren't superior to minerals."

"Not even angels?" I said sarcastically.

"Especially not angels," he exclaimed laughingly.

Chapter 15

You need to understand something at this point. I NEVER get up early, if I don't have to go to work and don't have some other kind of appointment. In fact, there are many Sunday mornings that I have faithfully attended St. Simmons of the Beauty-Rest, Church of the Divine Mattress.

Nevertheless, I once again found myself wide awake the next morning, ready to greet the dawn.

This time it seems that the majority of the heavenly host decided to sleep in. The vocal accompaniment came from one lone figure, standing on the easternmost corner of the roof, silhouetted by the sun. The one voice was enough though, very similar to one of the soloists that you hear performing with boys choirs.

It wasn't until later, at breakfast, that I found out that the beautiful voice actually came from Celeste.

Amazingly, the effect was the same. Even with only the vibration of that one voice, the patterns and colors still changed and swirled.

As it was ending, I realized that Gabe was again with me.

"Another perfect day," I said slowly, in awe.

"But then again, they all are, aren't they?" he completed, with a rich chuckle. "I see you're really starting to pick up on the perfection of it all."

I turned to him, "Is that why you use that greeting, to help others learn to see the perfection? To help us appreciate it all?"

He actually seemed to blush a little. "Well, sort of. It's really to remind me, too. It's sort of an affirmation for me."

"You never cease to amaze me," I told him. "I would never have thought of an angel needing an affirmation to keep him thinking positive."

"It's a bit more than positive thinking," he explained.

"Think about the words carefully. Then think about how powerful words and thoughts are."

"'Another perfect day' claims the beauty and abundance of universal perfection for the new day." He spoke passionately. "And 'But then again, they all are, Aren]t they?' extends the claim beyond today, to all days, and then encourages the listener to join in with the vibration.

"In the Judeo-Christian tradition, all of Creation was spoken into Being. That's almost literally true. In reality, it wasn't so much the Creator moving lips and expelling breath to form words. No, It sent out Its thoughts, Its energy, and the vibrations of that energy formed everything that ever existed.

"Our words, and our thoughts, have that same power. They're energy too. They have vibration and that vibration becomes the reality that we experience.

"I told you that we're the same, and I meant it. We all create our realities with our thoughts and words. After all, what is prayer?

"Prayer is putting our desires, our needs, and our gratitude into spoken or thought energy. That energy goes out into the universe and becomes our reality."

I had to ask. "Then God does answer every prayer?"

"The Creator answers every thought, word, and deed. We may not like the answer, but everyone is answered."

"When I said 'God'," I pointed out, "you said 'Creator'. Is that what we should call Him or Her?"

His reply surprised me. "You can call It 'The Great Pumpkin', if you want. The Creator is just that, the Creator of it all. As for that 'him or her' stuff, pure energy really isn't male or female, that's why I say 'It'."

"In fact, I had hoped that all of your shape-shifting yesterday would've helped you realize one important thing. That is, energy beings, whose form and characteristics are based on vibration, really don't have any permanent gender."

With that, his features became more feminine and his body shape changed.

Gabe, now I suppose Gabrielle, continued, "I am that same energy, with only a slightly different vibration. See what I mean, Mister It's-Fun-To-Be-A-Tree?"

He then changed back into the Gabe that I was used to.

"That's why theologians over the centuries finally had to break down and say that angels aren't male or female. We just confused the heck out of them."

He paused for a second and put his hand on his chin, as if pondering something important. "You know, maybe that's the one thing they actually got right!" he laughed.

"I suppose you all got a big chuckle out of the debate over 'How many angels can dance on the head of pin?' too." I offered with a grin.

"Well, that is why this resort is where it is," he replied.

"Sort of an angelic pun, if you will." He then did a little soft-shoe step.

I had to think for a second, but then I got it. "Pinhead Buttes Resort. Dancing on the head of a pin!" I said, shaking my head.

After breakfast, we went out into the garden and I asked Gabe how Celeste's solo had had the same effect on the sunrise as the whole choir had the day before.

"Simple," he explained, "what you saw was your perception, on both occasions. Her vibration, or that of the whole ensemble, would have had no effect at all to someone who wasn't open to it.

"It's like I told you before, what you see, hear, feel, or whatever, is based on your tuning your vibration to produce the patterns that make it perceptible to you. In other words, you see what you want to see, and you hear what you want to hear."

I had to ask, "Then what would someone who wasn't tuned into it have seen?"

"Whatever they wanted, of course," he said, as if it should have been obvious. "Or at least whatever they believed they would see. They might have even seen a dull cloudy sky, if they were psyched up for the disappointment."

"But I didn't believe that I'd see what I did in advance. I was completely surprised, not to say awed, on both days."

"Maybe consciously, but deep down inside you were ready and willing to create those images in your mind. You must have been, you saw it."

"So, what did you see then?" I prompted.

"Perfection. No doubt I would have seen something totally different, but just as perfect, had I been observing on my own," he said blandly. "But I was tuned into you and your vibration. I wanted to experience it from your point of view."

"So if that was the reality that I created for myself, why didn't I know that it was going to happen? Why did it surprise me?"

He faced me and put his hands on my shoulders, like a parent who is about to try to explain something very complex to a young child. "Because you knew, deep within you, that you needed to see it. You knew it in the same way that you knew to come here at all. You knew that you were ready for what you'd experience here. You knew at the spiritual level."

After pausing for a few seconds, he smiled and said, "Don't worry, you'll understand before you head back home. You still have a couple days more to understand the secrets of the universe."

Slowly he closed his eyes and turned his face upward. I expected either for him to say something profound, or for a miracle to occur. Instead, he said, in a loud commanding tone, "Don't even think about it!"

Then I heard grumbling from above and looked up just in time to see the 'Blue Birds' grumpily turn and fly to the other side of the courtyard.

Chapter 16

"I want to show you something interesting," Gabe said. "Let's go outside."

He led me out of the garden, through the lobby, and out the front door. At the bottom of the steps, we turned to follow the wall of the building around to the southeast side.

As we turned the south corner of the building, I was surprised to find that the hotel was not built on the top of the mountain at all. The highest point was actually a hill about one hundred yards southeast that rose another thirty feet higher than the site of the lodge.

Seeing my surprise, Gabe explained, "The hotel wasn't built up there because the peak was too small for it. We did find a good use for it though, as you'll see."

Winding around the side of the hill was a path that seemed somehow familiar. When we were about half way up, I suddenly remembered from where.

"This reminds me of the Tor that's described as being on the Isle of Avalon in the Arthurian legends," I commented, "the processional path spiraling around the hill, leading to a Druid temple at the top."

"Very good," Gabe replied. "That's how we designed it, although you won't find any Standing Stones up there."

The day was warm, and the exertion from climbing the hill made it even more so, but the path was shaded by trees and there was a cool mountain breeze to make the hike most enjoyable.

When we reached the top, I had expected to find a rounded hill or flat clearing. Instead, there was a circular indentation, like a bowl, about sixty feet across with a perfectly flat bottom about six feet below the rim.

Leading down from where we stood at the top of the path to the floor of the crater was a set of stone steps. Three similar rock stairways were also evenly spaced around the circle.

Gabe had said not to expect to find Standing Stones, but what was on the floor of the crater was almost more amazing. It was a large tile labyrinth, like the one I had seen in pictures of the Cathedral of Chartres in France.

Gabe, as usual, seemed to be enjoying my surprise. "Well, what do you think?"

"It's beautiful," I replied, a little out of breath from the climb, "but why is it here?"

"It's a tool for our guests. When a person walks the labyrinth, it helps them to focus, to remember. Besides, it was either this, or a tennis court.

"Have you ever walked a labyrinth before?" he asked.

"No, but I've seen pictures of them."

Just then another angel, one I hadn't met before, landed a few feet away and folded his wings.

As he walked over to join us, Gabe said, "This is Albert. He's going to help you with your walk. I'll catch up with you at dinner."

With that Gabe opened his wings and flew off toward the lodge.

Albert was slightly over six feet tall, with sandy blonde hair and radiant green eyes.

"Ready for your little stroll?" he asked.

"Are you the Albert who was outside my window the other morning?"

He grinned. "Yeah. We take turns doing that to the guests on their first day. Partly because it breaks the ice for them, and partly because it drives Thomas crazy."

"Most of the folks who come here are advanced enough for it not to bother them, especially if they've already gotten through the revelation part.

"Ready to go for your walk or do you need to rest a little longer?"

I was still recovering from the climb, so we stood looking out over the labyrinth for a few more minutes. As we did, he explained how it worked.

"A labyrinth isn't a maze, it just resembles one. Actually, there is only one path into the center, and no side trips or dead ends.

"You can walk it as fast or slow as you like, and you can stop to rest or meditate any time you want. In short, there's just no wrong way to walk it.

"When you get to the center, stay as long as you want, then take the same path back out.

"Occasionally, one of the members will decide to walk the labyrinth. I do it fairly often myself. If someone does come around, don't worry about them. This is a totally individual exercise, and whatever they are doing should not affect you, or your walk.

"In that way, it's rather like your life span. You do both on your own, however you choose to do them, and, in the end, you end up where you started."

After he finished, I stood looking out over the labyrinth for another minute, admiring it.

If you have never seen one, labyrinths are things of simple beauty. This one was round, with eleven layers of switched-back paths radiating out from the central rosette. It was laid out in polished tile, the paths done in saffron with dark purple separating them. From above, it reminded me of some ancient, mysterious petroglyth, or of a crop circle done in stone.

When I was ready, I walked down the steps to the starting point.

Albert followed me until I reached the entrance to the path. "Just take your time, relax, and be open to whatever comes to you."

I took my first step into the labyrinth, half expecting to be transported off to another world. After all, I've always associated the word "labyrinth" with mazes, legends of monsters, and the stuff of Dungeons and Dragons. Nothing happened.

I took another step, and then another. There was no grand revelation, no flash of insight.

"Well," I told myself, "you're only eight feet into it. What did you expect?"

I walked on and began to look at the path. Albert was right, it was like life. When you're involved in it, when you concentrate on it, you lose the bigger picture. You see just the portion of the path you're in. When I looked at only the section of path I was on, I could no longer see the pattern of the whole labyrinth.

The path seemed to go on forever, but I found I wasn't bored with it. Every turn, every step allowed me to look at the whole from a slightly different angle. A study in perspectives? Oh, how the view changes when you look at it from a slightly different angle.

Finally, I reached the center rosette, a space shaped like a flower with six small round petals. I slowly turned to view the whole labyrinth from the center. It stretched out in all directions. I had reached the destination, but still had to continue my journey.

I was at the center of this life, this labyrinth, with all the twists and turns of my path surrounding me, bringing me to where I was. Next, I had to visit them all again, look at them from yet another angle.

As I worked my way back along the path, I once again thought about the pattern. Each segment, each turn was part of the whole pattern. Each segment could be experienced individually, but there was only one path that flowed through it all.

Could the labyrinth symbolize more than just one life? Could it also symbolize the one energy that flows through all the myriad of lives that make up the pattern of reality? Could each turn be like one of the lives that this path, this energy flows through?

As I came back to the starting point, I was deep in thought. Albert said nothing. He just smiled.

There was a bench at the bottom of the steps and we went over to sit down.

After a few minutes, he asked, "How was it?"

I was still a bit pre-occupied and mumbled something.

"Sounds like you had a good walk. Feel free to come back whenever you like. Believe it or not, every walk is different."

We got up and started up the steps. On reaching the top, I turned to walk down the processional path. After going only a few steps, I realized that Albert was gone.

I looked around to find him, and saw him flying off toward the lodge. At the same moment, I could hear his voice say, "I thought you could use the time to think."

I thought about it for a second and then said, "You're right. Thanks."

The figure turned in mid-air and waved.

I walked back to the lodge, knowing that I had remembered something important, but not knowing just yet how important it was.

Chapter 17

As I reached the top of the steps at the entrance to the lodge, I noticed a grandmotherly lady standing on the porch off to the left. She had a gentle smile on her face, but her eyes were moist, as if she had been crying.

I turned to walk over to her, but she didn't seem to notice me. Instead, she was staring off into the distance.

It wasn't until I followed her gaze out to the west, that I discovered what had her so enraptured. It was a simple, fairly plain, sunset. Nothing special, no choirs of angels. Just the sun falling below the mountains, without even a cloud in the sky to add texture.

I stood near her for a few minutes, trying to understand what she saw that had moved her to tears. But it was still a mystery to me.

I was still watching the last of the light on the horizon when I heard her say in surprise, "Oh, my! Hello, dear. I didn't hear you come up. I was just so involved with the perfection of it all."

She dabbed at her eyes with a lacy handkerchief. "Did you enjoy the labyrinth?"

"Why, yes. How did you…"

"Oh, fiddle. Haven't you done the revelation bit yet? You do know who we are, don't you?" She grinned.

"Yes, ma'am. It's just that…"

"You can't get used to us knowing what's what. Well, I'll tell you a little secret." She leaned over to whisper in my ear, "You know more than you think you do, too.

"And don't call me 'ma'am'. My name's Ariel."

"Ariel?" I said in wonder. "Aren't you Clara's friend?"

She smiled broadly. "Did Clara mention me to you? I sure miss her being here. Maybe I'll slip off later and go visit her."

"Ariel, if you don't mind, what was it about the sunset that was so moving to you? I mean, it was a pretty plain one, no real magic."

She looked out to the west again and sighed. "Perfection! I saw only perfection."

She turned abruptly back to me. "Why, what did you see that wasn't perfect?"

I didn't know how to answer that. "Well, sure it was perfect, but..."

"But it wasn't special." She interrupted. "It wasn't magic. There weren't enough clouds or colors or texture.

"Have you been listening to Gabe, or not? It's all just perfect, because that's the way it was made. That's the way we were all made, perfect.

"Would you like to see what I mean? Do you really want to know what I saw in that sunset?"

"Yes, of course I do," I replied without thinking.

No sooner had the words left my mouth, than I saw the sun rise quickly back up out of the west, hover for a second a few degrees above the horizon, then begin its slow descent once again.

This time I was watching it from another perspective, her perspective. I was Ariel!

I saw the fiery ball of the sun moving through space. I felt the spin of the earth and knew the forces involved in keeping it in its orbit around the sun. I was touched by the wonder of what it took to put this all in place, to literally think it all into existence.

As I watched, I began to reach out and feel the vibrations of all the other creatures that were within view. I soared with a hawk that was hunting for an evening meal. I swayed with trees, and savored the last rays of life giving sunshine for that day. I could feel the energy that flowed within each plant and animal and stone. I was one with the perfection of all creation.

As the sun finally disappeared, I was myself again, but still I felt moisture in my eyes.

"Now you know the perfection," Ariel's voice said softly.

When I turned to thank her, she was gone.

Instead, Clarence was standing by the door, smiling gently.

"'My! People come and go so quickly around here'," he said. He knew that I'd pick up on the quote from 'The Wizard of Oz'.

"You *are* into movies, aren't you, Clarence?" I was still recovering from Ariel's gift.

"Seen 'em all!" He chuckled. "It's sort of my hobby. They're so much like reality."

He opened the door, motioning me inside. Then I followed him over to the conversation pit, and we sat down.

"Movies have stories that express the realities of the characters. You can see their emotions. You can feel their pains and triumphs. All the while you know that it isn't real, it's an act. Harrison Ford isn't Han Solo, nor Indiana Jones, nor Jack Ryan, even though he played those parts.

"The funny thing is that, for the duration of the movie, within the reality of that story, he was those characters."

"But that's a contradiction, isn't it?" I asked.

"No, it is just like reality. Each of us is a spirit, an energy, if you will, that has taken on an individual form. Indiana Jones was just a part that the entity Harrison Ford took on temporarily.

"Harrison Ford did not end with the closing credits. He just quit playing that character. Neither will the entity, who's playing Harrison Ford, cease to exist when the character Harrison Ford leaves the screen."

I was starting to see. "So you're saying that our current lives are just a role that the spirit within us is playing?

"Then is reincarnation real, or are we all just one-part players? What about sequels?"

He smiled broadly, "Oh, no, you don't just play just one part! As for sequels, each character you play experiences what it needs to while it's on the screen. You may play a similar part in some other flick, but each role you play is unique in one way or another.

"Movies are like lives in other ways too. I think that's why I enjoy them so much. Watching a movie is like watching people imitating the Creator. They select a story, prepare a script, and build a set. The real difference is that movie actors get to remember the whole story throughout the filming. While living a lifetime, you know the story, but you don't remember how it comes out or even what happens in the next scene."

I had to mention another difference. "But scenes in movies aren't shot in order. They're only put in the right order in the cutting room."

"Yes, that's another similarity. Don't act surprised. You were already told how irrelevant time is. What makes you think that things actually happen in any certain order?

"A philosopher once said that time existed so that everything didn't happen at once. Deepak Chopra, in the 'Way Of The Wizard', said something similar; that time was created so that we could get the benefit of each individual experience.

"Well, that describes why time exists, but it doesn't really explain its nature. Time is like a script."

"A script?" I asked, astonished.

"Sure, all the incidents of the story are in the script. They're all there together, but to be meaningful, they have to be read in a certain order.

"Like you said before, the scenes of a movie aren't filmed in the order they appear in the finished version. The editor takes each clip and puts it together in the right order to tell the story. He does that based on what it says in the script.

"When you hold the script in your hand, you hold the entire story. Not only that, you hold the one thing that determines in what order the audience sees the events in the movie."

I could see his point, but had to ask, "So who wrote our script? Was it the Creator? I thought we were all supposed to have free will. Is everything we do predetermined?"

"You wrote it," he explained. "Before you were born, you determined the purpose of your life. You came into this life with a plan for what you would do and experience. And like any good movie director, you can change the script whenever you choose. That's what free will is all about."

"How can I change the script? If I planned this all but, why would I include bad things?"

"Think about any movie you've seen. If everything went smoothly, if there were no challenges, two things would happen. First, it would have been boring and, second, the characters would not have had any opportunity to learn or grow."

"You planned the challenges in this life, and how you would handle them, as learning experiences. Each incident, good or bad, is an opportunity for growth. Everyone in creation is the same way, going to school."

"Only in this school you are both the student and the teacher. You take the tests, but they are tests of your own devising. You plan out the course and then teach it to yourself."

I wondered out loud, "What about angels? Are you in school, too?"

"Actually, yes, we are. But we're more like teacher's aides than students. We're here to learn, but we also know your lesson plan and help you through it when you need us."

"As for how to change the lesson plan, all you have to do is decide to change it. After all, it's your script. If you don't like how it's playing out, just make up your mind on how you want it to be. Once you believe in the change, give it energy through prayer or affirmations, and then watch it happen."

Chapter 18

"Chow time!" Gabe said, as he stepped into the conversation pit. "How was school today?"

"Great! Perfect!" I enthused, knowing that I had a lot of homework to do. "I just have to absorb it all."

"Yeah! You looked a bit overwhelmed. But don't worry, you're doing fine."

"Let's go eat!" he said, rubbing his palms together like a greedy child. "Will you join us, Clarence?"

"Oh, my, certainly," he sputtered. "Yes, thank you, I will."

It was then that I noticed how he changed. When he wasn't teaching some great cosmic truth, he was just like the character from the movie. But when he was teaching, he was confident and eloquent, just like Gabe.

After eating, Clarence left us and I decided to ask Gabe about this.

"Angels are just like humans," he explained. "Each has their own personality."

"Clarence may lack some of the confidence that others have, but he's just as capable as any other angel I know. In some ways, he is more capable because he has a real talent for expressing things in simple, understandable ways.

"He also knows himself well enough to overcome his confidence problem by tapping into the source that we all have access to."

"What source is that?" I asked. "Do humans have access to it too?"

"Sure you do!" he exclaimed. "I'm talking about the great pool of cosmic knowledge, the energy that flows through all of creation.

"I suppose that if Clarence was to explain it, he would use the Star Wars term 'The Force'. But there's more truth to that concept than even George Lucas knew when he wrote about it.

"Let's just say, for now, that it's the same creative energy that formed the universe. It's the same intelligence."

He looked at me for a minute and then suggested, "You've covered a lot of ground today. Let's take the evening off. How about a nice hot soak in the Grotto?"

"That sounds perfect!" I said, obviously relieved. And then we both laughed.

I went to my room and changed into my swimsuit.

Gabe was waiting at the elevator across the hall from my room. At the second floor, Celeste and Anna joined us, also on their way to the Grotto.

When we got to the basement, we walked along a hallway that was just as ornate as those on the upper floors. Doors led off on both sides of the hall, presumably leading to the bowling alley, gymnasium, and other facilities that Lawrence had mentioned on the first night.

At a point that seemed to be directly below the lobby we came upon, was a descending cast iron spiral stairway, very ornate, with golden handrails. This completely filled a perfectly circular shaft that was carved into the rock below the hotel.

As we descend, I couldn't help but notice how smooth the walls of the shaft were. They were like marble, but you could see each of the layers of rock. I knew that some of the rocks were too soft or brittle to polish, but the surface was still flawless.

After descending through about thirty feet of rock, the stairs broke into the open air of a cavern.

The ceiling was about twenty-five feet high. Both it, and the floor, appeared to be made up of natural rock formations.

The cavern was lit with various colors, by light sources hidden behind some of the formations, and extended off into the darkness in two directions. A small river wound its way from one end of the cave to the other, filling the air with the relaxing sound of flowing water.

At one point the river widened out into a calm pond that was also fed from both sides by small streams of water. At various places, I could see other streams also making their contributions to the flow.

I couldn't tell where most of the streams were coming from, but many were obviously the overflow from several pools that sat steaming throughout the cavern.

In the dim light, I could see figures relaxing in the pools and in the pond. One was alone in a large pool about 15 feet up river, and waved for us to join him. When we got closer, I could see that it was Clarence.

"How's the water?" I asked him.

"Oh," he sighed, "just heavenly!"

This caused everyone within earshot to start laughing, and we joined him in the 'heavenly' warm mineral water.

After we had settled in, Anna asked me how the lessons were going.

"Alright, I guess," I started, rather distressed by what I thought was my slow progress. Then I noticed Gabe's disapproving expression, and corrected my statement to, "Perfect, just perfect."

Gabe smiled, nodded approvingly, and then started to laugh.

The next few hours were filled with joking and splashing, mixed with periods of quiet relaxation. Everyone seemed to have a good time, even Thomas.

He had joined us in the pool, shortly after we arrived, saying that I looked like I could use another human around for "mortal support."

In the elevator on the way back upstairs, I asked a question that had been on my mind ever since the first day.

"Gabe, why do angels need this place? I never would have thought of angels eating meals, or lounging in hot tubs, or any of the things humans do for relaxation.

"I've been told about the stresses and pain of your jobs, but why all these creature comforts? I thought angels were above the physical pleasures."

He looked at me for a minute, then smiled gently and said, "For the same reason you enjoy them, of course.

"Like I told you before, we're very much alike. You're in the physical form, living a lifetime, in order to learn, to experience. Other than that, we're both beings of energy."

"There's no reason that one being of energy shouldn't enjoy the same pleasures as another.

"The fact is, there are many things that are best experienced in a physical form. Like the feel of warm water, still pulsing with the energy of the earth, fresh from a hot spring; the taste of fresh vegetables, gifts of the soil and sun; and the warm vibration of laughter, a sound as glorious as any choir of angels.

"We come here to refresh our spirits, to balance our energies, and to relax. The same reason, as I recall, that you were originally headed for that resort down the road."

I felt a bit foolish for having asked those questions, but, after he finished, the gentle smile on his face showed that he understood my curiosity.

"Get some rest," he said, as I turned and started down the hall to my room. "We have of a lot to cover tomorrow."

Chapter 19

The next morning, I found myself in the observation tower once more. As I stood enjoying the cool mountain air, waiting for the daily miracle, I said to myself, "Another perfect day!"

I was half surprised when Gabe didn't appear behind me and finish the phrase. Instead, I was there alone, looking out toward the east as the sky began to lighten.

On the far corner of the hotel's roof, I could make out three figures.

"Aw," I thought, "today's sunrise will be accompanied by an angelic trio."

As the sky grew red and the glow of the approaching sun made each cloud gleam golden against the dark blue sky, I saw the patterns begin to form and swirl. This display was turning out to be the most spectacular I had seen.

And the music was not the choral perfection of the previous days, but rather was a mesmerizing series of tones. Not vocal, nor any instrument that I've heard before.

It was more like a melodic version of the ringing you sometimes get in your ears. Yes, like that, but not the same. Instead of a constant whine, the tone separated and harmonized with itself and with the visual patterns that formed before me.

As the sun broke above the mountains, the patterns and tones reached their climax and then faded away.

I started to applaud in appreciation of the spectacle and looked across to the opposite corner, but nobody was there.

"Lose something?" Gabe asked from his usual perch on the railing.

"Where did they go?" I sputtered, ignoring his normal abrupt appearance. "There were three angels over there, just a second ago. They were singing so beautifully."

"Singing angels? I didn't see any angels." he said, with a mocking sound of disbelief in his voice. "And they were there just a second ago?"

I looked again at the now empty roof, then back at Gabe.

"They left just after they knew you'd seen them. You did this one all on your own."

"What are you talking about? The patterns! The music! I didn't do that!"

He looked at me with a big smile, waiting for me to calm down.

Finally, he said softly, "Yes, you did.

"It's like I've been trying to tell you all week. Everything you see or hear or experience is based on your vibrations interacting with the world around you.

"Sure, the first two mornings, the other voices helped you along. But beyond that, it was all your doing."

I pointed across the garden. "So what were they doing there this morning?"

Still calm, Gabe explained, "They were there to reinforce your expectation. You wanted music and a light show. You mistakenly equated singing angels with getting that show. Celeste, Anna, and Albert stood there just long enough for you to start your expectation in that direction. Voila, the morning miracle. And it was all your doing!"

This last he said while poking me in the chest with his finger for emphasis.

"But HOW did I do it?" I whined.

"Don't tell me we have to start all over again," he said, with more than a hint of frustration creeping into his voice. "Do the words 'beings of energy' and 'vibrational Patterns' sound familiar?

"Ok, I'm sorry. You just don't remember this yet," he said, calming himself.

"Did you ever have something happen that you knew would happen? Or did you ever want something so badly that you could taste it, and then you actually got it?

"Did you ever have things you needed just fall into your lap? Find money when you were broke? Meet just the right person to help you with some project, at just the right moment?

"Have you had something happen to you that seemed bad at the time, but turned out to be for your benefit in the end?

"Sure, you have. And you probably wrote them off to good luck, or God looking out for you, or a Guardian Angel, or even serendipity. Well, that's all true. It's all of those things.

"But do you know how they all work?

"They're all within you. It's your energy that draws them to you. You put out the vibration that creates the things you want. You set up the conditions to put you in contact with the people you need. You even arrange for the challenges in your life that make you grow and learn.

"It was your energy and your vibration, guided by your expectation that created the miracle you just saw.

"You don't have to know how it works. You just have to know that everything, every one, is made of energy. That energy has a vibration, and each vibration interacts with every other vibration.

"When you expect something to happen, that expectation becomes part of your vibration. That vibration goes out into the universe and draws back what you expect.

"You'll notice that I didn't say desire or want; I said expect. That's because you have to know that it's coming. You have to know that it's going to happen. You have to expect it for it to become part of your reality.

"That's why you saw the patterns and heard the music. You expected it, and it happened."

He paused, so I asked. "But why was the music so different, so ethereal?"

"Because this was entirely your music, no outside influences. It was a creation of your vibration. It was the unique music of your personal universe. Now that you've heard it, you can expect to hear it again."

Chapter 20

The breakfast crowd was unusually quiet that morning. Conversations were hushed. There were none of the outbursts of laughter that were so common when the members gathered anywhere.

I could feel the change even before we got to the restaurant. In fact, I noticed a mood shift in Gabe while we were still in the elevator.

At first, I thought that it might have been some lingering frustration from our earlier discussion. I dismissed that idea, however, when I thought about what I knew of Gabe's personality. He just wasn't the type to stay upset about something so minor.

As we left the San Miguel's, I finally asked what was going on.

"We just got some disappointing news, I'm afraid."

"News? Your mood plummeted while we were in the elevator alone." I momentarily forgot that I was talking to an angel. "What news would depress all of you so much?"

"Just more of the usual stupidity, that's all!" he grumbled. He continued to explain as we exited the lobby and walked out into the courtyard garden.

"Some humans are so ignorant of their place in the universe, so full of themselves and their beliefs, that they feel free to do anything they want to anybody at all. They think it's just fine to cause death and destruction just because of ethnic or religious differences."

"You would think that, if they really believe the teachings of the faiths that they claim to fight for, they'd see that none of them encourage this foolishness. Jesus, Buddha, Mohamed, none of them suggested that killing a neighbor was the pathway to heaven."

Yes, he was definitely upset. I decided that it would probably be wiser, if not safer, to let my angelic friend calm down a bit before asking what had happened again.

We made it all the way to the central fountain and sat silently on one of the benches for several minutes before he finally continued more calmly.

"I never did tell you the news, did I? Well, the leader of one group of impoverished people decided to grab the meager resources of his neighbor. The carnage lasted for only a few hours, but resulted in several hundred human deaths, and tens of thousands among the other animals in the area.

"Now that leader can proudly say that he has control over another village, the scorched earth under it, and enough food to feed his army for about three days. What a waste!"

I thought about what he had just described and realized that he could have been talking about almost any battle in any war in human history. Suddenly hearing it from a different point of view made it seem all the more stupid.

I felt ashamed of our species. I just sat staring at the fountain, not wanting to look into Gabe's eyes.

He finally sighed deeply and continued, "Sometimes I just don't know what the Creator had in mind when It started all this, but it sure is a lousy way to run a universe. Maybe I'll just quit."

"Quit?" I said in disbelief. I turned to find him smiling widely at me.

"No, I can't quit. Who would they get to teach folks like you the secrets of the universe?"

We both laughed uproariously. I was surprised by how much better I suddenly felt. It seemed that his depression and anger, as well as joy, were somehow contagious.

Tragic as this news was, it brought up an interesting question. "If angels are beyond time and space, and if death is not an ending, why do angels care about the death of a human or any other creature? If who we are is eternal, why would those deaths upset you so?"

His reply started out slow and cautious.

"There are things about angels that you don't understand yet. Actually, they're part of the few differences between angels and humans that we have already discussed, but you may not have really grasped the significance of them yet."

"What did I tell you was the biggest difference between us?"

I was up for the quiz. "That I didn't remember who I really was. Other than that we were both beings of energy with different vibrational patterns."

I was rewarded with a broad smile. "Give that student a gold star! That is exactly right."

"Now, what have you learned about all things in the universe?"

"The same thing. It's all made up of energy, with each thing having its own frequency and pattern." This was too easy. There had to be a trick question coming, some grand "Gotcha."

"OK! What else? What other relationship is there?"

"Oh, you mean 'The Force.' The energy that links everything."

"Excellent! That's your answer. I knew you would remember it by yourself. What do you want to do with the rest of your time here?"

He was up and starting toward the path back to the lobby.

"Wait a minute!" I jumped up and followed him. "What do you mean? 'The Force' is the grand secret of the universe? I don't understand! What was the answer to my question?"

He turned back with a smirk. "Gotcha! Be careful what you expect, or you might just get it!"

I shook my head in disbelief as I watched him return to the bench. "That's what the world needs, a smart-aleck angel!"

I sat next to him and he continued. "Humans don't remember their nature, that's true. They also don't remember other things too."

"One of the most basic things they don't remember is that interconnection. That 'Force,' if you will."

"Angels, on the other hand, are constantly in touch with that connection. To us, it's as strong as any of your senses. That's how we knew what had happened, and is also why we felt so strongly about it.

"We actually felt the pain, the hate, the despair of the event while it was going on. When someone dies, we feel their fear and their pain. This is just as natural for us as the act of dying is for the person, so we can bear it.

"But when the pain and death and destruction are so senseless, well, even angels have their limits."

I could see he was getting upset again, so I changed the subject.

"So what about this connection? Does anyone else but angels feel it? How about humans, can we learn to feel it too?"

"Some of you already do, if you are open to it. Close your eyes and I'll show you.

"Now open them just a little bit. Just a slit. Can you see everything as clearly as when your eyes were open?

"Now open them wider. You see more and more clearly. Now open them completely. Better, right?

"That is just how it works with your connection to the universe. The more open you are to it, the more you'll perceive.

"The fact is, no humans are shut off from this connection. They all just have different degrees of awareness to it.

"Psychics, prophets, gurus, and lunatics are probably the most open to it."

"Lunatics?" I said in surprise.

"Sure, many of them are the most open to the universe. The problem is that their minds are not ready for it. They have the knowledge, but they aren't prepared to cope with it.

"Actually, that's the reason for the whole forgetfulness thing. You don't remember the full truth because it would interfere with the purpose that brought you here, the lesson you came to learn. You couldn't cope with the lessons of this life if you had to carry around the memories and feelings of the universe with you all of the time.

"Animals, on the other hand, are constantly in touch with their connection. That's how instinct works. For instance, how they know when a storm is coming. They sense it through their connection.

"Most humans are only minutely open to it, so they call it intuition, or a hunch."

I was intrigued. "So how does this connection work? How would you describe it?"

"Love! Universal Love."

"Do you remember what you felt the other night when you first saw my wings?"

"Yes, even though I was overloaded by the reality of it all, I felt a warmth, a love. I felt safe; confused, but safe."

"You were feeling that connection," he said with a chuckle. "It's the energy of the universe and It's passion for Itself.

"You've heard the phrase 'like attracts like'? Well, that's true with universal energy, universal Love.

"Thomas told you about how angels feel about you. He was right, but he didn't explain it completely.

"Angels pray for, and help, and weep over humans because it's natural for us. It's the natural result of our total openness to the connection between us. We feel what you feel, and we also feel the love energy between us. We have to care. We have to help. We just can't stop ourselves.

"Would you like some examples of how it works, how it feels?"

"Sure!" I replied, expecting another of our unusual learning experiences.

"Remember how it felt to be a tree, or a bird, or a rock? Remember how you felt after touching the perfection of an otherwise dull sunset from Ariel's perspective? Remember how the mood of me and the other members affected your mood?

"That's what it's like to be an angel."

Chapter 21

I was still sitting on the bench, deep in thought about the last lesson, when I heard several gentle thumps on the grass behind me.

Gabe had excused himself a few minutes before, saying there was something that he needed to go get.

I thought the noises might have been Gabe returning, but when I turned around, I saw the whole 'Blue Birds' squadron folding their wings and walking toward me.

"You're going to get drenched!" I warned myself, realizing that I had probably looked pretty somber from the air.

Celeste giggled. "Peace, man. We're out of ammo. Everyone was so down this morning that we had to go double up to hit everybody who needed it."

"Go 'double up'?"

"You know," Anna explained, "like Padre Pio used to do."

I must have still looked puzzled, which seemed to amuse them.

I started to ask again, when they pointed up over my head. I looked up just in time to see another group, made up of identical twins to the angels in front of me, let loose of a dozen or more water balloons.

"Bombs away!" the Celeste above me shouted.

"OH, YEAH!" squealed her twin on the ground, as every balloon scored a direct hit on me.

Both groups broke into gales of laughter, which grew even stronger when I tried to act like I was upset. I finally couldn't hold in my amusement anymore and ended up having to sit down, I was laughing so hard.

As the merriment died down, I looked up at the still airborne group and witnessed yet another amazing sight.

While I didn't know where the second flight of 'Blue Birds' had come from, or how they could exist, for that matter, it seemed normal to me that they would just fly off now and wreak havoc somewhere else in the garden.

Instead, as I watched, each being wavered, began to glow, and then shrank quickly into a melon-sized ball of white light. These moved through the air until they were hovering above, and slightly in front of, their counterparts on the ground.

In the meantime, Anna, Celeste, and the others had partially unfurled their wings. Each of them then reached up and cupped their hands around the still glowing orbs in front of them.

They stood that way for a few seconds, reminding me of statues that I had seen in the shopping area of Caesar's Palace in Las Vegas. Then the balls of light faded into nothing.

Celeste folded her wings. She then turned to watch as the others flew off.

When they were gone, she took my hand and led me back over to the bench. She seemed to know that, in addition to being drenched to the skin, I was still confused about what had just happened.

"If you don't mind," I started, "could you please explain what I just saw and how you all duplicated yourselves like that?"

"Oh, that was what I meant when I said we had to go 'double up'. That way we can cover twice as much ground in the same amount of time."

"But how?" I stammered.

"That's easy. Like Anna told you, Padre Pio and other humans have been doing it for years. It's just a matter of ignoring the 'artificial laws' of space and time."

"But if they're laws, how can you just ignore them?" I was still confused.

"I said artificial laws. They were made up in the human mind, not written in stone by the finger of God."

"No, the 'laws' of the physical sciences that they teach in colleges are just how human scientists have decided that the universe works, based on their own observations. What does that tell you?"

"Well," I ventured a guess, "they saw what they expected to see. That's because it was their vibration that created the conditions that they were observing in the first place."

"Very good." She smiled. "But in addition to that, the results were also affected by the mass vibration generated by the group belief system of their community."

This surprised me. "You mean what I see and experience can be affected by people around me, in addition to my own vibration and expectations?"

"Sure! Your neighbors all put out a vibration too. If they all believe the same thing, that aspect of their vibration will harmonize and strengthen the vibrational pattern.

"That's how things like 'mob mentality' and 'mass Hypnosis' are explained. Each member of a group sees, hears, and believes what the group does because their vibration is being tuned by the synergy of the group's collective belief. As more people pick up the vibration, it gets stronger. The stronger it gets, the more people are drawn into it.

"Nazi Germany was a good example of this. So is just about every riot or war that you see on the news.

"Getting back to 'going double up', that's the term we've taken to using to describe being present in two places in space at the same time."

"But how can you do that?"

"Easily! You know that time and space are just dimensions. Dimensions are just measurements that you use to define the limits of your personal universe.

"Time keeps events in some linear order that you can understand, and space deals with the physical part of the illusion.

"Now, you can accept that you can exist in more than one position in the dimension of time, right? Otherwise, you would be around for a split second and then you'd be gone.

"Well, if you can be in more than one place in the dimension of time, why can't you be in more than one place in the dimensions of space at the same time?"

I thought about that for a few seconds. "Logically, that makes a lot of sense, but I still don't see how you would do it."

"Listen, don't worry about the 'how' part too much. It's just like everything else, once you accept it into your reality, once you expect it to happen, it does.

"It's all very easy for us. We don't have to remember our true nature, overcome any personal or cultural belief systems, or get over lifetimes of limitations in the physical world.

"What you should concentrate on while you're here is your belief system and your expectations. Everything else will follow."

Just then, Gabe came strolling up carrying a towel.

"Figured you might need this," he said, tossing the towel to me and winking at Celeste. "Has it been raining out here?"

"Thanks. You missed all the fun," I said, as I started to dry off. "I won't ask how you knew that I'd need this. I'll just be appreciative and assume that it's what you went off to get."

Celeste got up and started to spread her wings. "Anything else I can help you with, before I go catch up with the 'Blue Birds'?"

"Yeah, one more question, if you've got a moment." I still wanted an explanation of the energy balls.

"That ceremony you did, with the glowing spheres, what was that all about?"

"Not a thing, but did you enjoy it?"

"Well, yes, it was beautiful. But what do you mean by 'Not a thing'?"

Gabe piped in, "Did you guys do that Luminous Sphere routine of yours again?" He turned to me. "You're right! That is so pretty."

Celeste gave a slight curtsy and replied, "Oh, thank you! You are too kind. But like I said, it was nothing, quite literally nothing."

I didn't believe it. "But what was it then?"

"Just a little pageant to entertain ourselves and you. 'Doubling up' and 'undoubling' doesn't require all of that hoopla. We just thought you might enjoy a little spectacle with your shower."

Chapter 22

Gabe had also brought a small knapsack back with him. "Want to go for a little hike?"

I followed him to the corner of the building opposite the lobby. There we found a metal door of the type that normally would have a lighted red EXIT sign over it.

When we stepped out through it, we were on the gently sloping "valley side" of the hilltop.

The tree line was about 100 feet away from the building and about 20 feet lower in elevation.

As we walked down the slope toward the trees, I could see that the ground suddenly got much steeper a few yards after you entered the trees. There was, thankfully, a path that ran along the rim of the drop off and seemed to provide for an easier decent.

After we had walked about a half-mile, quietly enjoying the sights, sounds, and scents of the forest around us, I noticed something interesting. This path, like the one that led up to the Labyrinth, spiraled around the mountainside. This allowed for a gentle descent and, more importantly, ascent, without the use of switchbacks.

When I mentioned this to Gabe, he explained, "You know, this path was here when the resort was built. I think maybe the local natives used it, and the peak, for some sort of ceremony."

I thought about it for a few minutes. "It's interesting how often spirals and circles appear in nature and religious symbols."

"That's because it's a natural representation of how energy flows," he replied. "Take an electric circuit. The energy flows from pole to pole, but only when the circuit is complete."

"Electrons orbit around the nucleus of an atom, moons orbit planets, planets orbit stars, and stars orbit a galactic center. Each of these objects is a sphere, a three dimensional circle. Each is a manifestation of energy.

"Every culture that's ever existed has sensed this and included it in their sacred ceremonies and symbols. From the Tibetan Buddhists, with their prayer wheels, to the Celtic stone circles, like Stonehenge, and carvings of spirals. Even the religion of the American Indians had their Sacred Hoop and Medicine Wheels.

"And did you ever notice that most dances involve either people dancing in a circle or people revolving around each other," I added.

"The point is," he continued, "humans instinctively recognized the circular patterns of energy in the universe and include it in their art and religion."

"Speaking of religion," I decided this was a good time to ask one of my many big questions, "which one is the right one? Most say that theirs is the only true one and that everyone who believes differently is damned to some kind of punishment. Who is right and who is wrong?"

"I thought we went over this already." He thought for a moment and then shrugged. "Well, maybe not. All of them..." he started, but paused for a second.

I stopped dead in my tracks. "What? How can that..."

"and none of them," he continued, ignoring my outburst.

"All of them have some essence of the truth. Each is based on the founding culture's way of viewing reality. Each is exactly what its followers were ready to believe and be faithful to."

"So why do the religions of a culture change?"

"Because the needs of the people change. Something new arrives that needs explaining. Or maybe the religion of a different culture seems to explain the mysteries of life better than the old one did."

"Take, for instance, the Tibetans. They were a warrior culture, with an empire that spread throughout Asia. Then along comes Buddhism and the culture changes. From then on, they've become probably the most peaceful people on earth."

"On the other hand, you really can't say that the religion of any culture has changed. Usually, if a culture has a predominant religion and it changes significantly, or is replaced by another, the old culture disappears and is replaced with a new one."

"That's why the true believers of any faith would rather die than allow another faith to coexist with theirs. They know that it would mean the end of their culture, their world."

This raised another question. "Then religious hatred is really based on fear of cultural changes?"

"To some extent. That explains inquisitions, book burnings, and witch-hunts. But it also explains fear of any new ideas. New thought might affect the comfortable status quo, so it must be stamped out, along with anyone who supports it. You find that everywhere."

"So how do some religions survive and thrive, even in different cultures?"

"Well, first off, when a new religion becomes part of a culture, the culture changes enough to be considered a new one. But for a religion to survive, it must change too.

"Christianity is a good example. When it became the official religion of Rome, by Imperial decree, the people resisted it. Their culture was based on a religion that worshipped a whole host of gods and the people were comfortable with what they knew.

"In fact, to the dismay of the Christian officials, the people still tended to observe their familiar 'pagan' holidays."

"So what was the answer? Just adjust the Christian holiday schedule to coincide more closely with the Pagan one. That's why Christmas is celebrated when it is, because it coincides with the Roman Saturnalia.

"Another, more modern, example is the changes made in the various Christian sects to make worship more convenient, or more acceptable, to their followers.

"The Roman Catholics did this by changing the language of the Mass, turning the altar around, and allowing a Saturday afternoon Mass to count as Sunday attendance. Those were changes to make the religion work within the culture, thus changing both."

This looked like a good time for another big question. "Some people look at that kind of change as sacrilege, as evil. Is there really such a thing as good and evil? Is there a Devil? Is there a Heaven or Hell?"

"Yes, there is evil," was his abrupt answer, "and there is a Devil, but they aren't what most people imagine them to be.

"Everything has two sides to it. Oriental philosophy calls it Yin and Yang. In reality, it's a very complex issue, because every aspect of each of us has two sides to it as well. We all have within us male and female, enlightened and ignorant, good and evil.

"At one time or another, we all exhibit both sides of every aspect of ourselves. Yes, I know what you're about to ask, even angels.

"Good and evil are probably the most difficult aspects to deal with, however, because they're largely dependent on the culture that they're being viewed from.

"For example, if you were the member of a tribe that practiced cannibalism, you would be perceived as evil if you didn't chow down on someone who was being served as part of a ceremony.

"On the other hand, from the perspective of a European Christian, those who joined in would be damned to an eternity in Hell's fires. Even so, he would have no problem killing and eating most other animals, just not another human.

"Who is good and who is evil? Well, the cannibal and the Christian are both good and evil. They both have their good and evil sides.

"So what about the action? Was eating his neighbor right or wrong?" Gabe paused, waiting for me to reply. He looked around, and found a rock to sit on while he waited.

Reaching into the knapsack, he pulled out two water bottles and tossed one to me.

I thought about it, based on what I'd already been taught. Finally, I had to admit, "I don't know. Who am I to judge?"

"Exactly!" He jumped up and slapped me on the shoulder. "Let's head back."

"But what's good, and what's evil?" I now begged, following him up the path.

"I don't know, either," he responded, laughingly. "Remember the old saying; 'Judge not, lest ye be judged'? Truer words were never spoken."

I couldn't believe this. "You mean there are no rules, no guidelines? What about murder? Surely, this Creator cares about that? Or child molesting? Or genocide?"

He stopped and turned to me. "The Creator cares more than you know. It feels every pain, every emotion that each and every creature in the universe feels. It experiences every death, every abuse."

"The duality of each aspect of every creature is the essence of 'free will'. It allows them to learn and grow. The thing is, in the cosmic scheme of things, none of the things that you mentioned have a lasting impact.

"Besides, another aspect of free will is that you plan out the general path and mission of each lifetime before you begin it. When you enter a physical body, you know, and have agreed to, how you will die, and what you will do and learn until then."

I was reaching overload here. "I don't know why I'm here, and I sure don't know how I'm going to die! Wait, wait, I know what you're going to say; I just 'don't remember it'!"

He smiled calmly. "That's right, you don't. Besides, since you have free will, you can totally ignore the plan and do something totally different."

"I can?"

"Sure, we all can. The problem is, you came here for a reason. You have something to do, something to learn, something to experience. Although it may be of minimal importance in the overall plan of the universe, it has to be done. If you don't accomplish it, you'll always feel incomplete, like you've failed at something. You'll go through life with a feeling of being lost."

"And what happens to people like that, do they go to Hell?"

He laughed, shaking his head. "No, that is their Hell. It's a hell of their own making. After they die, however, they just come back and try it again. They must do what they came to do, no matter how many lifetimes it takes."

I was still puzzled. "So I get in my car. I drive down to the nearest convenience store and hold up the place. As I leave, I shoot the clerk and everybody else in the store, men, women, and children. That's just fine, then?"

"It's not what's in your life plan, but you would be acting in 'free will'.

"In that case, you would be accessing what we'll call, for lack of a better term, the darker side of your free will. That's what evil is, turning from your plan to do something destructive."

"But if we don't remember our life plan, how do we know when we are straying from it? How do we discern good and evil?"

"Before you take any action that you're not sure of, tune in to your higher Self. Tap into that connection with the Creator. Ask yourself if you're doing the thing that you were meant to do, and if you're doing it in love."

"How do we tap into that connection?"

"Meditation, prayer, it's up to you. Maybe it's sitting on a rock in a place like this." He pointed around him at the forest and the scenery visible beyond it. "Sit in a quiet place and ask. You'll know."

"So there is no Devil, no fallen angel, trying to lead us into evil?"

"I didn't say that. What I did say is that there are two sides to every aspect of our beings. That includes a dark side of each of us, which rebels against our mission. And, no, there isn't some guy with a pitchfork, horns, and pointy tail."

"People who do the things that you brought up earlier, they follow that side of their being. They feel only the hate side of the love/hate aspect, and they choose, at least in this lifetime, to run away from the Creator."

The thought of demons suddenly came into my mind. "You keep telling me how alike we are. Are there angels that have chosen that darker side, too?"

He hung his head in sadness. "There have been some. They've been known to try to disrupt things, but never with any lasting effect. They are usually quickly escorted from the scene. This is, of course, a part of their free will."

"Let's go back to that convenience store in town." I changed the subject back to one he was more comfortable with. "What about the victims? Surely it wasn't in their life plan to be killed by a crazed gunman?"

"Well, actually, it usually is. Nobody dies whose plan didn't call for it. There are no meaningless deaths."

"But that's not logical!" I was confused again. "If it wasn't in my plan for me to shoot them, how could it be in their plan to be shot by me?"

"When something is within your plan, or when you change something in your plan, the universe conspires to make it happen."

"Remember, time and space are illusionary. If something planned is going to happen, all the circumstances needed for it to occur are put into place to bring it into reality. The right people are in the right place. The traffic lights change at just the right time. The sun shines or the rain falls. All this creates just the right conditions for the event."

"Now if someone changes their plan, the same thing happens to bring everything into perfect position for what they now want to do. Even if the change is a spur of the moment thing, the event is reverse engineered in time to bring all of the required players into the right positions under the right circumstances."

I was in awe. "Sounds like quite a feat of choreography!"

"Not when you view it from a place outside of the dimension of time. It just happens."

"So how much room does free will give us to change our lives without screwing up the plan?"

He smiled. "Quite a bit, really. Besides, if you change it in a spirit of love, the plan will actually adjust to your desires."

"For instance, say your plan called for you to be a low to middle class factory worker, but you wanted to do something that required you to be well off financially. If your purpose was productive, not to hurt someone else, and you approached the universe in a spirit of love, your plan would alter to lead you there."

"What about the rest of my path, wouldn't I have to come back to finish those lessons?"

"Not necessarily. Many of the lessons and experiences you would have had could be altered to fit into the new situation. The remainder would be fit into other lives, as need be. The key here is your intent."

"Much of what you spend lifetimes learning is about intent. If you act in love and truth, you have learned the key lessons of any lifetime. If you live by hate and fear, you'll just have to stay after school."

We were approaching the top of the path now, but I had one more question. "Gabe, if our life plan is so important, if we already know the lessons we are here to learn, why do we forget it all when we're born? Why go through all of this to learn something you already know?"

"You don't actually go through your life to learn anything new. You just go through it to experience it from the perspective of a unique set of circumstances."

"Remember what I told you about vibrational patterns and perspective?"

I nodded.

"Well, each life you live has its own unique perspective on events. Over your many lifetimes, you may experience similar things, but always with a slightly different point of view."

"This fresh perspective is very important, and is protected by the fact that you forget everything about your true nature when you arrive. That way you're free of the memory of all of your past lives and ready to experience everything as if it were the first time."

Chapter 23

I walked the rest of the way back to the hotel in quiet contemplation. In fact, I was so deep in thought that I paid no attention when Gabe didn't follow me into the garden after he opened the door for me.

It wasn't until I heard the giggling from overhead that I even noticed where I was.

"Some people just gotta learn to lighten up!" I heard Celeste say, in a mock preaching voice, as the 'Blue Birds' flew off, leaving me standing there dripping on the path.

Actually, this second drenching of the day was rather refreshing after the warm sunshine and the exertion of our hike. I even seriously thought about feigning depression to get another dose.

"So, the shower in your room isn't working?" I turned to see Clarence standing on the path a few yards away. "Or have the 'Blue Birds' just made you their special project?"

"Oh, I don't know," I looked after them, "they seem to mean well. Besides, it felt good this time. Have they ever hit you or Gabe?"

"Me? Oh, yes, several times, but never Gabe. They wouldn't hit anybody who wouldn't appreciate it. And Gabe would not."

I was wondering where Gabe had disappeared to, when Clarence asked me a startling question, "Ready to start flight training?"

"What? Are you kidding? I'm not an angel! I don't have any wings! I can't fly!"

Clarence looked at me with a slightly disgusted frown. "Oh, piffle! Like I told you before, you don't need wings. You just have to expect that you can do it."

"But you angels use your wings to fly. How can I do it without them, if you can't?"

In answer, he rose into the air without opening his wings, and landed right next to me.

"We don't need physical wings either, we just like the way we look and feel with them. Besides, most humans wouldn't believe who we said we were if we didn't have them.

"Sometime I'll have to teach you how to manifest them for yourself, so you can give it a try that way. You did notice that we don't have them all of the time didn't you?"

I told him that I had, but just thought that they hid them.

"Oh, no, no! How could we hide something like wings? We manifest them when we want them. We create them. You could do the same thing, if you really wanted to.

"Anyway, let's get started." He rubbed his hands together. "First Ground School!"

"OK," I said, trying to sound positive, even though I was scared to death.

"First off, there's nothing to worry about. You just have to remember what you know about reality, that you create it for yourself."

I started to challenge this, but he continued, shaking his finger at me. "No, just listen for a minute.

"You manifest everything in your reality by expecting it. You attract the people and things you want and need to you by giving them energy. You do it by knowing, even if only subconsciously, that they are already there.

"There are actually three types of flight to learn about.

"The first is the one that you see when you watch an eagle or one of the members here in the aviary. That's physical flight, involving wing shape, and lift, and such. To do this, you would have to manifest wings and know that you can overcome gravity.

"It's fun, but you can fiddle with that later.

"The second could best be referred to as teleportation. This is where you decide to be there, so you are. It requires that you step out of one position in time and space and into another.

"It's much quicker, in linear time, but is still a bit advanced for you.

"The last is simple levitation."

"Simple?" I interrupted.

"Oh, certainly. You just have to let go of your belief that your body is being held to the ground by gravity. Or, if you like, you can believe that you can float on air, that you are as buoyant in air as you are in salt water."

"But how can I do that?" I complained. "I'm not filled with helium!"

"Remember, you create your reality. What, in your universe, tells you that you can't levitate?"

"The law of gravity, if nothing else!" I was getting frustrated.

"Well, it's your reality. Repeal that law. There wasn't even such a thing as 'The Law of Gravity' until Isaac Newton. What would your excuse have been before him?

"No, you decide. It's your reality. You make the rules."

"But I can't...," I started again.

"Baloney!" he interrupted. "You've seen people lay on nails, haven't you? You've seen people walk on hot coals?

How do they do it?

"I'll tell you. They change their reality. They believe the nails won't pierce them, the coals won't burn them. If you made the decision for yourself, you could do those things too."

"But without wings..." I objected.

"No, they're not needed. Not for this type of flight!

"Think about a bumblebee. Human scientists agree that it's aerodynamically impossible for bumblebees to fly. But they do, because it's not impossible to them.

"Now, are you ready to quit whining, and start flying?"

"I'll try," I said skeptically.

He smiled, then his face transformed into that of Yoda, from the Star Wars movies. "Do or do not! There is no try!" he said in a gravelly voice.

"Ok! Ok! Point taken." I chuckled as he turned back into himself. "Let's do it!"

"That's more like it." He beamed. "Now sit down on that bench and close your eyes."

"And think wonderful, beautiful thoughts, while you sprinkle me with pixie dust," I jokingly added.

"If you think that would help you," he agreed, seriously. Then he smiled.

"Ok, close your eyes and relax. First, we're going to alter your belief system. It's just simple meditation. I'll lead you through it. In the end, though, it's up to you to alter your own reality." His voice had become soft and soothing.

"Now concentrate on the top of your head. They call that your 'Crown Chakra'. It's your best contact point with the energy of the Creator.

Concentrate and open yourself up. Open up to truth, to your higher self.

Picture yourself bathed in energy. Not an energy from somewhere else, but from within you. It's the energy of the Creator that runs throughout Its creations. It's an energy of love and power.

Accept that energy. Accept the control of your reality. Accept the Creator within you.

Now, take a moment to feel your ownership of your universe. Feel your connection with everything and everyone around you. In your mind, trace back along this connection, along this energy link. See how and why you brought them into your life. See the circumstances and the reasons.

Relax even deeper now. Good, good!

Reach down and feel the earth below you. Explore your connection to it. Find the vibration that you call gravity. It ties you to the earth. It's important to your human existence. See it as elastic, something you can stretch, something you can play with.

Experience the vibration of the air around you. Feel it as a fluid, as something thick and warm and heavy. Know that, like water, it will support you. You can float on it. You can rise up on it. You can even swim in it.

Now allow the elastic gravity to stretch out and allow your body to float up in the air, like a kite on the wind. See yourself floating up, drifting off of the bench. Rising into the warm, thick, supporting air."

I was totally relaxed and no longer felt the bench that I was sitting on. This was the best guided meditation I had ever done.

With my eyes still closed, I could see myself rising higher off of the ground. It was one incredible illusion. One that I wanted to be real.

"Now," he continued, very softly, "slowly open your eyes, but look only straight ahead."

I did as he said and found his face just inches away from mine.

"Stay relaxed, but know that you did this for yourself. You created it in your reality." He was smiling broadly.

I was curious about what he meant, but caught a glimpse of movement off to my right.

I turned my head to see Anna and Celeste smiling, and hovering in mid-air, their wings moving slowly.

Beyond them, I saw the glass elevator rise up level with us and stop. Albert entered it and waved as it started back down.

"How do you feel?" Clarence asked, his voice still melodic and calm.

"Great!" I replied. "Like I'm floating in a pool."

Celeste chuckled, "Now that's what I call lightening up!"

It was then that it really struck me. "Wait, a minute! I really am flying!"

"Floating, actually," Anna chimed in. "Flying involves, you know, moving around."

"You think you're ready for that?" Clarence asked.

I took stock of where I was and how I was doing. I wasn't sinking and I wasn't panicky.

I was actually quite comfortable.

I finally said, "Sure. What do I do?"

"It's easy." Celeste said. "Just decide where you want to go and decide to be there."

I thought about the central fountain and decided that I would like to see it from above.

Nothing happened.

"What am I doing wrong?" I wondered.

"What did you decide? Where did you decide to be?" Clarence asked.

"I want to fly over to the center of the garden."

"Oh, no, you have to decide to be there." He explained, cheerfully. "Wanting it is not enough. It's like getting up in the air in the first place, you won't get there until you know that you're already there."

I thought about how I got airborne. I closed my eyes and decided to be over the center of the garden. I felt myself moving, so I opened my eyes and found myself moving backwards across the garden, about twenty feet above the ground.

Suddenly it occurred to me, "Just how high is the fountain?" I asked myself. "About fifteen feet, if I remember right. So I should be alright."

I heard someone shout, "Look out!"

I turned my head to look behind me, in the direction I was traveling, just in time to see the approaching branches of the fruit tree on top of the fountain.

I instantly decided to be about six feet higher and shot up, missing the upper branches by only a couple of inches.

"Don't worry," Clarence said calmly, as he joined me in floating above the fountain, "you just need some practice. You'll get the control part figured out.

You can do this anytime you want, now that you know that you can. At least as long as you continue to know that you can," he added somberly.

"What do you mean, Clarence?"

"Sometimes people lose faith in their abilities. They listen to what the world tells them is possible, instead of what they know is true.

Just remember today. Know what you did here. Don't let anyone steal it from you, no matter what." Then he continued, more cheerfully, "Why don't you go play with the 'Blue Birds' for a while? You can use the practice."

"Thanks, Clarence," I said, looking around for the others.

"Just fly facing forward and keep your eyes open," he called as I moved away.

On my way to join Celeste and Anna, I happened to notice a lone figure, deep in thought along one of the trails.

When I told the 'Blue Birds' about him, Anna replied, "We'll see about that!"

They handed me two water balloons and we started toward our prey.

He was standing at a spot on a path that had a splendid view of a waterfall that flowed into a large pond.

"This is your first raid," Celeste whispered to me, "and you found the target. You go ahead and take the lead."

"Thanks!" I said, and turned to start my run.

We were coming in low and fast, following the path, so as to hit him from behind.

"No! Abort!" I suddenly heard Anna yell.

I turned my head to look back at them, but they had all stopped and were floating stationary in the air. When I looked forward again, I realized that I was still moving very fast, about seven feet above the path.

Our target, on hearing Anna's cry, had turned to face me. It was Gabe, and he didn't look amused.

It was at this point that I lost control and began losing altitude. Gabe saw what was happening, but still didn't have time to jump out of the way.

I hit him about chest high, with both water balloons bursting on impact, and together we tumbled into the pond.

Anna and Celeste landed to help us climb out of the water, but Gabe didn't seem too happy with any of us. He just turned his back and stared off into the distance, refusing to speak.

We all tried to apologize to him, but he didn't even acknowledge anything we said.

I was devastated. After all that he'd done for me, all he'd taught me, I'd spoiled our friendship with one thoughtless act.

I decided that maybe it was time for me to leave. I couldn't see any reason to stay if I wasn't going to have any more lessons with Gabe. I turned and started slowly toward the elevator.

The sound started as a low rumble, almost a growl, but quickly grew louder and more recognizable. It was a chuckle, deep and joyful. I turned to find Gabe hovering above us, now laughing out loud.

"That devil!" Celeste said to me. "See, he was only pretending to be mad!"

Suddenly, he had something in his hand. It was a fire hose that stretched out behind him, fading into thin air.

"No," he chortled wickedly, "I don't get mad. I get even!"

With that, he turned on the water and thoroughly dowsed all of us.

Chapter 24

After going up to my room for a change of clothes, I met Gabe and Clarence for dinner.

Apparently, my little flying lesson had become the news of the day, especially my crash landing into Gabe.

All during dinner, Members kept dropping by the table to say hello, and pat me on the back. Many of them I had never met before this.

Afterwards, Gabe suggested that we head up to the observation deck.

"You're still not mad at him?" Clarence asked, pretending to be concerned. "Throwing a student off of a building is pretty harsh punishment, even from you, Gabe."

"You're the one who taught him to fly and then sent him to play with the 'Blue Birds'." Gabe replied. "Come to think of it, maybe you're the one that should be tossed off the roof."

They both began to laugh and we all headed for the elevator.

When we got up to the roof, a truly magical sight greeted us.

I've seen and appreciated the beauty of many a night sky, but the mixture of cool, thin mountain air, the lack of any city lights, and there being no moon, made this one extraordinary.

This must have been the kind of night sky that inspired Carl Sagan to come up with his famous "billions and billions" phrase for describing the number of stars. Each was so bright and sharp that you would have thought you could reach up and touch them.

I slowly walked around the deck, taking in the amazing beauty of it all. After making one full circuit, I stopped a few feet from Gabe and Clarence, but couldn't bring myself to take my eyes off of the amazing view.

Clarence had been watching me fondly and finally chuckled softly, "You never could resist a starry night sky, could you?"

"No." I sighed absently. I suddenly realized that my mouth had been stuck open in a silent "Wow!" ever since we'd arrived.

Still staring at the sky, I continued. "So how do you know me so well? You aren't going to tell me that you're my Guardian Angel, are you?"

"No," he said gently, "I just looked back over your path. I hope you don't mind, I just wanted to know you better."

This actually made me take my eyes off of the sky. "What do you mean, back over my path? Do you mean you can see into my past?"

"Sure, why not?" Gabe answered, rather impatiently. "Don't tell me that you're thinking of time and space as real again?"

"Into your past and future," Clarence replied, ignoring Gabe's comment. "When your view is from beyond time and space, you can be conscious in whatever time and place you choose.

I can look back over your life because I can choose to be conscious of the various times and places that you've experienced along the way."

"You can do it too," Gabe added. "In fact you do it all the time. It's called memory."

"But I thought memories were stored in the brain," I protested.

"Just think about this logically," Clarence continued. "You already know that humans, like angels, are really beings of energy having an in-body experience. Right?"

"Ok," I admitted. "I've got that."

"Well, these currently-human energy beings may not remember it, but they still have access to all of the knowledge, all of the power, that any other energy being has. They're still connected to the Creator's energy system.

Subconsciously, they still tap into information that is far beyond their current earthbound limitations. Some do it more frequently than others and are called geniuses."

"You don't really believe that you can hold the memories of every detail of your lifetime in the small blob of tissue between your ears, do you?" Gabe added.

"Well, I've also heard that we store memories in the tissue of other parts of our bodies." I suggested.

"If you think about it," Clarence explained, "does it really make sense to store the information at all? I mean, if you have access to the event as it's happening, why watch the video?"

"Here, try this," Gabe offered. "Pick a memorable event from your past. Now close your eyes and go back to that moment. Don't just think about it. Be there. Remember every sound, every scent, every feeling."

"Are you there? Are you in that moment?"

I was. I had chosen my wife and my wedding day. I was in the church. I felt the nervousness. I smelled the flowers. I was there in that moment.

Then I heard a voice in my right ear, "Over here."

I turned and looked along the communion rail, toward the side door of the church. There stood Gabe and Clarence, wearing tuxedos just like the one I wore.

I opened my eyes and was back on the roof of the resort, back in that place and time.

"You see," Clarence continued, "you weren't just accessing the some biological data storage system in your brain, you were there and then. You were in that moment, as much as you are in this one, here and now."

"If not, how do you explain our little visitation?" he smiled.

"So, while I was there, what happened to me here and now?" I wondered. "Did I just cease to be?"

"Not at all," Gabe explained. "You accessed that time and place. You didn't travel back there. Your current physical body was sitting here with its eyes closed, experiencing its linear, physical reality."

Clarence picked up the idea. "It's a bit like using a computer to look at somebody's page on the Internet. You don't actually go to China, you just access what's on their computer at that time and place."

Gabe looked at him with admiration. "Now that was a turn-of-the-millennium explanation, if I've ever heard one. Well done!"

Clarence took a little bow. "Thank you very much. I try to adapt my examples to the lifestyles of our guests."

"So, when I remember something, I'm actually experiencing two different positions in time and space at once?" I interrupted.

"Yes," Clarence started to reply, "Well, consciously. Actually, your true self, the energy being that you really are, not being limited to space and time, is experiencing all places and all times simultaneously."

"You just experience the one lifetime in a linear fashion, one place, one moment at a time, because of the limiting filters your conscious mind imposes on you."

"Without those filters, you just couldn't experience the one life, and each of its lessons, without an infinite number of distractions."

"But doesn't knowing all of this add quite a few distractions, too?" I asked. "How do I go back to living a normal life, having the experiences and learning the lessons, when I know the truth about it all?"

Gabe walked over and put his hand on my shoulder. "You can, and you will, continue this lifetime's lessons because it's in your plan to do so. You will continue to consciously live one moment at a time, in one place at a time.

"You will, however, know more of the truth about your Self than you did last week. You'll know that you have access to an infinite pool of knowledge, and to infinite power."

"You always had access to those things. You just didn't know it consciously."

"More important," Clarence added, "your knowledge of your true nature should help you to cope better with your lessons as you experience them on a moment by moment basis.

The key is that you have to strive to get the most of each of these lessons. To do that, you have to be fully present in each and every moment of your lifetime.

Don't worry about eternity. It will be there for you after school. Just do what's right, right now."

"So, what good is enlightenment then, if it doesn't change anything?"

"Enlightenment?" Gabe laughed. "Enlightenment is like having someone hand you a lantern, so you don't trip in the dark on your way to the outhouse. The path is the same, the lantern just helps you see the obstacles a little better.

"What we teach you isn't meant to replace the lessons you took on human form to learn. No, you came here to be shown what lies beyond your current existence. Our job is just to remind you of who you are, and how you fit into the whole of creation.

Your job, your life, is to experience and learn from whatever your life path includes. Enlightenment, if that's what you want to call your lessons here, changes nothing."

"There's an old Buddhist story about enlightenment,"

Clarence suggested, "That sums it up nicely. A young student, searching for the truth, came across an old man on the road. The old man was bent over, carrying a heavy load.

"The student looked at the older man and recognized him as an enlightened Master. So he asked, 'Please tell me about enlightenment.'

"The old man thought for a second, then laid down his burden and stood up perfectly straight.

"The student said, 'Ah, I understand. But what comes after enlightenment?'

"In answer, the old man simply bent over, picked up his burden, and continued down the road."

Chapter 25

That night I had a terrible time getting to sleep. I kept thinking about how little time I had left with Gabe, Clarence, and the others.

Sure, I missed my wife. But how often would I get an opportunity to learn the secrets of the universe from real angels?

What was I doing wasting this precious time lying in bed? Shouldn't I have been up, learning from them, asking questions, every possible minute that I was here?

There are monks who spend their entire lives meditating, searching for the kind of information that I was getting here this week. How did I rate? Wasn't there something I should do to prove myself worthy of this enlightenment?

After all, this was my last night at Pinhead Buttes and I just knew that I still had a million things left to learn. How could I possibly sleep?

"Just shut your eyes, relax, and stop thinking so much,"

Gabe's voice said from the darkness of my room. "You're doing just fine."

"Gabe?" I asked, squinting to find him. "Are you there?"

"Just go to sleep," his voice replied. "You learn better when you're rested."

"And don't worry about getting up for the sunrise," Clarence's voice added. "We'll hold it for you."

Suddenly, all my questions were forgotten, and I was very sleepy. I dozed right off.

When I woke up, I turned on the bedside lamp and looked at my watch. I was surprised when I saw that it was almost nine, since the room was still very dark.

Just then, I heard a tapping sound at the window. I got up and pulled aside the curtain, seeing Albert hovering outside the glass.

He pointed toward the roof and said, "Whenever you're ready." Then he waved, and flew upward and out of sight.

It was then that I remembered what Clarence had said about holding the sunrise for me.

What had he meant by that?

I quickly dressed and ran up to the observation tower.

Gabe was waiting in his usual morning spot on the railing.

"Glad you could make it," he said, in a tone of mock annoyance. He then pulled a ridiculously large watch from his pocket, one about the size of a schoolhouse wall clock.

"Tsk, tsk," he continued, looking at the watch. "And you were the one who was so worried about time."

"But how?" I was amazed. "Sunrise should have been hours ago."

"Maybe where you live," Clarence said, suddenly standing next to me, "but we just might be in a different time zone."

Gabe turned the watch so I could see its face. It read 5:45. "We'll talk about it later," he said, pointing off to the east.

Conscious of what I had been taught about my connection with the universe, I decided to allow myself to feel the Love that flowed through it all. This time I opened myself up to the wonder and perfection like I never had before.

In my very soul, I became one with the clouds and the sun and the mountains. I played in the vibrations of the light, and reveled in the patterns that formed as it interacted with my own energy.

I felt all of the joy and awe that I had on previous days; in fact, even more so.

As the sun rose above the mountains, I returned fully to myself, knowing that it truly was "another perfect day, just like all of the others."

I turned to find Gabe and Clarence, now joined by Albert, Celeste, and Anna, watching me with broad, loving smiles. I assumed that they had tuned in to what I had just experienced, and I was glad that they had.

After a moment, Celeste broke the silence. "See what happens when you let 'em sleep in?"

Chapter 26

"So you're leaving today?" Celeste asked, as we all left San Miguel's after a late breakfast.

"Pretty soon," I sighed. "I'm supposed to meet my wife in Dallas around seven this evening. Then we'll fly back to Tulsa together.

"I sure appreciate everything you've done for me. I've learned so much, and really enjoyed being here."

"Well, at least," Celeste responded, "you haven't been boring."

She glanced at Gabe and started to giggle. "We'll never forget your flying lesson. Will we, Gabe?"

Gabe tried to look stern, but broke into a grin. "I doubt it."

I looked around, at each of their faces. "Will I ever see any of you again?"

Celeste smiled, reached over, and laid her hand on my shoulder. "Don't worry, we'll be around. Even when you don't see us, you're always surrounded by angels."

"Sure, I'll know you're there." I smiled back, and then looked around the group again. "But I've seen you. How would someone who hasn't…? I mean, how can other people know that you're around them, helping them?"

Clarence smiled broadly, and broke into an imitation of W.C. Fields' gravelly drawl: "Feathas, ma bouy-o, feathas!" then said, in normal tones, "Angels let you know they are around by leaving their feathers lying around where you can find `em."

"Feathers?"

Celeste smiled at Clarence, shaking her head in amusement, but said to me, "Whenever you find a feather, or a coin lying about which seems to have come out of nowhere, that's an angel letting you know that they're around. And, that they care about you."

I stood for a moment, remembering the fluffy white feathers that I had noticed over the years, never thinking that they had any meaning at all. And, thinking of all the coins that I had found! I was amazed at how often the angels had been with me, and I had had no idea, until now.

"Come on, folks," Clarence chirped. "They still have some important material to cover." Then, to me, he said, "I'll catch up with you later."

I hugged each of them, in case I didn't see them again before I had to run. It was already eleven and I had to leave by noon to catch my flight.

As Gabe and I walked quietly through the garden once more, I was surprised that he didn't start his last lesson as we went. Instead, it wasn't until we reached the central fountain and were sitting on a bench that he began.

"So, tell me what you remember now?"

I chuckled. "So the final exam is an essay question then?"

"No," he grinned, "I just want to make sure that I know where you're at on your journey, before I help you get a little bit further down the road."

"Well, I know we're all energy beings experiencing our own unique views of the universe. Each of us experiences it differently because of how our individual vibrational frequency and pattern interacts with those of the beings and things around us.

The energy that we're made of connects all of us, and our Creator, giving us access to the power and knowledge of the entire universe.

Because this energy flow is outside of what we experience as space and time, we can step out of those dimensions and back into them, wherever and whenever we choose. The part of this that I am challenged by, is, how to do it."

Gabe started to reply, but I continued, "Also, since this energy flows through everything, all we have to do to really experience the point of view of someone or something else is to assume their vibrational frequency and pattern. Another trick I've yet to master."

"It's all of matter of your expectations," he interrupted, "and practice. You can also understand someone better by just tuning into their vibration, by just concentrating on them and opening yourself up to them."

He paused for a second. "Sorry. I thought you might like a little bit easier way of understanding other people's perspectives. Go ahead."

"Thanks, that sounds quite a lot easier. I can definitely use that.

Anyway, because we're energy beings, playing at being physical, we can manifest anything we want by expecting it to be there or to occur. That's how we create the universe that we perceive, by drawing the people, things, and circumstances to us that fulfill our expectations. It's also how we take on physical, and, at least in some cases, mortal forms."

Gabe was grinning broadly now, nodding his approval. "Go on."

"All of this is true of all beings put here by the Creator, even the ones that humans don't normally think of as beings. It's true of angels and humans, trees and birds, rocks and rhinos. The only difference between all of these things is their vibration.

"Why are we all here, experiencing our very own little perspectives of the universe? That's where my memory gives out, Gabe. Why do we need to come back, again and again, to learn these lessons of perspective? Is there some great cosmic scavenger hunt going on, with a collection of experiences that, when we collect a full set, we can redeem it for an eternity in Nirvana?"

I was frustrated. I'd learned so much, but seemed to understand so little of it all.

"Don't worry," Gabe said, obviously tuned into how I felt. "You're doing just fine. You just have one or two more things to understand."

"You seem to accept the idea of reincarnation for you mortal types. Right?"

I nodded. I guessed that he used the term mortal so as to include other 'living' things, like plants and animals.

"So, how does it work?" he prompted.

"A spirit, an energy being, is born again and again in different times. It lives different lives."

"Different times? But what is time?" He was leading me to some conclusion, but he wanted me to see it for myself.

"Well, time is a dimension, like the three dimensions of space."

"So, what does that tell you about reincarnation?"

A light was just coming on in my head. "If a spirit can be reborn in different places in time, and if time is just a dimension, then that same spirit could be born in different places in space but at the same point in time."

I was on a roll. "If that's true, anybody you meet could be the same spirit in another incarnation. Boy, that gives a new meaning to the idea of instant Karma."

"What do you mean?" he asked. I got the distinct feeling that I was on the verge of something important.

"If anyone I run into could be another incarnation of myself, anything I did to, or for, them, I would automatically be doing to or for myself. Instant reward or punishment, just not in the same mortal lifetime."

"What insights came to you while you were in the labyrinth?" he asked.

That surprised me. Why would he change the subject like that? I didn't answer for a second, so he continued.

"How could what you discovered about the labyrinth relate to what we're discussing now?"

"As I was reaching the end of it, I thought about how, even with all the twists and turns, there was only one path. It came to me that each little straightaway in the path is like each of the lifetimes that a spirit goes through. Many lifetimes, but only one spirit."

We sat silently for a moment. I'd just had a wild thought, but I was having trouble putting it into words.

"If the same spirit can be incarnate in more than one body in space and time," I proposed, "and if space and time are illusions, then that same spirit, that same energy could appear as more than one being anywhere and anywhen. It could even manifest as a being that is outside of space and time, like angels."

"Yep," Gabe chuckled, "just like angels. Go on. Just one more step and you graduate."

This was incredible. There was just one more logical step.

"Then you mean," I concluded, "that, since one energy being, existing outside of time and space, can manifest itself in any form, at any time or place it wishes, then all of the beings that have or will exist are actually that same being? There is only one energy being and that one is the Creator?"

He manifested a scroll of paper with a ribbon around it and held it out to me. "And here's your diploma. Congratulations!"

"But why," I sputtered, "would this Creator go through all of this? Why would It want to exist as this infinite number of beings? Why put Itself through all of trials and tribulations of life? Why suffer through the tragedies and pains? What's it all for?"

The diploma disappeared, presumably because I never reached out to take it from him.

"To be perfectly honest," he started slowly, "even I don't have access to the entire story.

What I do know is that the Creator is driven by an unquenchable thirst for knowledge. It manifests Itself into so many creations, under so many different circumstances, in order to experience those vibrations first hand.

In fact, since the Creator in each creature knows that none of the pain and sorrow is real, at least cosmically speaking, every creature is able to cope with whatever happens to them in their life. Each of these events, terrible as they seem to the participants at the time, is even less than a pebble on the road in the journey of the Creator."

"You know," I broke in, "my wife and I went to a Greek festival recently. One of the events was a tour of the Orthodox Church, during which the priest told us what he believed was the reason for God telling Moses that his name was 'I Am'. He said that it was because there was only one Being that mattered. That Being was God and everything else was just creatures created by God."

"A well informed man," Gabe commented thoughtfully. "At least, a very perceptive man."

"Gabe, if we can all access all of the knowledge in all of creation, how can you say that you don't know the whole story? Are there limits on the information we can tap into?"

"I'm not sure," he said carefully. "I have questions that I feel I should know the answer to, but don't. Where did the Creator come from? What is It like aside from Its creations? Does It exist beyond Its creations? Are there others like It?"

I thought about that for a moment, then offered an idea. "Maybe we are given access to any information that the Creator feels may be useful in our individual learning experience. Anything that It already knows, like Its own nature, that might just be a distraction to us, remains a mystery."

He smiled broadly at me. "Believe it or not, I never looked at it that way. Thanks, that makes me feel a little more content in my ignorance." We both laughed.

"Gabe, now that I know this, what am I supposed to do? I assume that I was brought here to learn this for some reason, other than just my own personal quest for meaning in my life. What's my next move?"

"That's up to you. It's your vibration, your lifetime. The Creator let us know that you were ready to be reminded of it, to be 'enlightened' as you called it. It's up to you what you do with it.

"Another thing to remember, though, is that everyone is the same. They all have the same capacity for remembering these things. In fact at a deep level, just like you did, they already know them, because the same energy of the Creator flows through them, too. Don't ever think that you are 'special' or 'advanced'. You were just ready."

I must have still looked confused, so he added, "Think about it. Meditate on it. The Creator within you will inspire you to do what is needed. Who knows, that inspiration may just suddenly appear out of thin air, just like magic."

"So," Clarence said, as he joined us on the bench, "until you know for sure what your next step should be, do like the old master on the road did. Just pick your burden up again and continue in the direction you were already heading. Just walk on."

That sparked a memory. "'Walk on'? Aren't those the legendary last words of the first Buddha?"

"So they are," he grinned. "What a coincidence! Maybe it's good advice."

All of this road talk reminded me to check the time, and I was shocked to find that I was now over an hour late getting started. I'd definitely miss my plane if I tried to "walk on" without using what I learned. At this point, I realized that I'd need help to do even that.

"Guys, I hate to go, but I'm going to have to literally fly if I am going to catch my plane in Portland."

They both smiled, but Clarence observed, "You'll have to fly so that you can fly?"

"I realize how silly that sounds, but I really need to meet my wife in Dallas. Do you have any better ideas?"

Gabe rolled his eyes back and said, "You just finished accurately describing the nature of the universe. You now know that you are, as is everyone else, a manifestation of the creative energy that made everything.

Yet you're worried about the time at which you have to meet you wife and the space you have to traverse to get there?"

Clarence looked at Gabe. "Be nice, this is still all new to him." Then he said to me, "Like the old Moody Blues song says 'Thinking is the best way to travel'. Why not just transfer yourself all the way to Dallas?"

"I suppose I could..." I began.

"But you're still having trouble accepting that you can," Gabe interrupted, bluntly, "let alone expecting that you can."

"Ok," I admitted, "I confess. I'm not sure I can do it by myself."

Gabe surprised me with a smile. "Good! You haven't developed delusions of being some sort of infallible deity. You can still admit to yourself and others that you have limitations, even if they are self-imposed."

"In that case, we'll help you," Clarence added.

"Otherwise we'd have let you figure it out on you own, just like in real life. You're still you, you just know a little bit more."

I was so relieved. "Thanks, what do I need to do? What about the rental car and my bags?"

Gabe chuckled. "We'll take care of the mundane stuff for you."

"You'll find that you never picked up the car in Portland and won't be charged for it," Clarence announced. "That's an example of reverse engineering. And your bag is already on the plane, checked through to Tulsa."

"Thanks," I said in awe, "what about my stay here. How much do I..."

Gabe interrupted, "It was our pleasure. You were our guest."

"Besides," Clarence chuckled, "we have very little use for money, anyway."

"Thanks, again!" I reached out and hugged each of them.

"Ok," Clarence said, his voice once again becoming soft and monotonous. "Close your eyes and relax. Focus your attention on your Crown Chakra. Open it up to the energy of the universe, the energy of the Creator. Feel your connection with that energy.

"Open yourself up to how that energy flows through you, how you are a part of that energy. Immerse yourself in the flow of the energy. Let go of this place and time. Let go of your physical existence here and now. Step out of those dimensions and experience the dimension of pure energy, pure Love. Experience your true self in that cosmic flow."

Gabe and Clarence must have been tuned in to my vibration, because even after I felt totally disconnected from the time and place that I'd just left, I could still feel their presence with me.

I felt, more than heard, Clarence continue; "Now place your attention on where and when you want to manifest yourself. It can be wherever you want, whenever you want. Put all your energy there and then. Concentrate. Picture your Self there. Know that you're already there. Expect your Self to be there. Be in that place and in that moment."

"Now open your eyes."

Chapter 27

As I looked around me, I began to laugh. Not just because of my amazement at suddenly finding myself seated in one of the uncomfortable chairs in the middle of the hustle and bustle of the Dallas-Fort Worth Airport, but because of what I heard coming from the PA system speaker over my head.

"On behalf of the staff, management, and members of the Pinhead Buttes Resort," Celeste's voice said in a cheerful but businesslike tone, "please let me be the first to welcome you to Dallas. It has been our pleasure to be of service to you, and we hope that, whenever you need enlightenment services, you will choose us again. Please have a nice evening in Dallas. And best wishes, wherever and whenever your Path leads you."

I pictured Celeste in my mind and mentally thanked her again.

Just then I sensed movement behind me and turned to see my wife walking toward me from the gate.

"Oh," she said, "you beat me here."

We hugged and kissed.

"How was your flight?" I asked.

"Long. How about yours?

"Different," I replied. "I'll explain later."

We looked at the flight schedule on the monitors and found that we had about an hour to wait and that our flight left from the next gate over.

"Great!" she said. "Where's that shop you told me about? The angel store?"

"That's a good idea. It's just a gate or two away and I wanted to thank Clara again."

As we walked down the concourse, she asked me about my retreat. I hadn't explained much of it to her over the phone. In fact, I was still trying to figure out how to put it into words.

"Well," I started, noticing landmarks that told me we were getting close to the right spot, "I had a lot of interesting conversations with some really different people. And I learned a lot."

"Ok. Like what? Who were they?"

I stopped and looked around, puzzled.

"What's the matter?" she asked, concerned.

"The store was right there," I said, pointing at a plate glass window that allowed a view of a baggage claim carousel on the other side. "I don't understand this."

"Are you sure this is right place?"

"I know it is. I wanted you to see it, so I was sure to take note of where it was." I turned away from her, looking up and down the concourse.

"Well, it's not there now. So, where…"

"Excuse me, young lady," a familiar voice interrupted.

"Did you drop this?"

I turned to see Ariel standing in front of my wife. She held out a gold necklace, with a small angel charm on it. At the same time she turned her head and winked at me.

"No, I didn't. Thank you, anyway. It is beautiful."

"Well, I think it would look good on you," Ariel continued. "You should keep it anyway. You can wear it when you travel again. It's Michael, and when you take Michael with you, you never know what good thing will happen to you. Right, Sonny?" This last was directed at me.

I just smiled, knowing that my wife had a real treat in store for her, and said "Oh, most definitely."

Ariel held out the necklace again, and my wife accepted it. Then Ariel pointed toward my feet and said, "Looks like you dropped something, too."

I looked down to see a blank white paperback book at my feet. I picked it up and my wife came over to look at it with me.

"What is it?" she asked.

I glanced up and saw that Ariel was gone, but didn't mention it. "It's a blank book," I said. "Who would publish a blank book?"

"It would have to be more intelligent than some of the stuff you read," she teased. "Are you sure there's nothing in it?"

I thumbed through the pages, starting at the back, but found only blank paper until I reached the inside of the front cover. There, written in black ink, was an inscription that explained where the book had come from and suggested what I should do next. It read:

This book doesn't have to stay blank.

Thanks for your company.

Enjoy the wings.

Clarence

Angels At Play

ABOUT THE AUTHOR

Michael Howard, while new to professional writing scene, has had a number pieces published in local publications. These include articles in school newspapers, as well as poetic and humorous contributions to military publications, while he was in the US Air Force.

An avid student of the spiritual, Michael is a voracious reader and can frequently be found attending seminars on various aspects of spiritual growth. His attitude toward personal growth is best summed up in one of his favorite sayings, "If you're not learning, you're not living."

Michael's material draws from a wide range of influences, since he feels that inspiration is not only to be found in the various holy books of the world. This is why you may find a reference to Deepak Chopra on one page and a quote from Yoda on the next.

From his over 30 years as a computer professional, Michael brings a new logical approach to his spiritual insights. As a fan of science fiction, he allows his mind to go beyond the accepted catechisms of today. And as a student of truth, he is not afraid to express what he has come to know.

Michael currently has two books in publication:

Angels At Play is a metaphysical journey to enlightenment. The book follows a visit to a resort called Pinhead Buttes, where all of the other guests are angels on vacation and the time is spent in mixture of fun and lesson on the nature of the universe.

Michael's darker side comes forward in his second book, The Unquenchable Thirst. This explosive political thriller explores how a second term president, with an excessive thirst for power, could remain in office after his term has expired.